Holidays on Ice

Holidays on Ice

by
David Sedaris

LITTLE, BROWN AND COMPANY

New York Boston London

Little, Brown and Company
Hachette Book Group
237 Park Avenue, New York, NY 10017
Visit our Web site at www.HachetteBookGroup.com

First edition originally published in hardcover by Little, Brown and Company, 1997
Second edition published in hardcover by Little, Brown and Company,
October 2008

"Seasons Greetings to Our Friends and Family!!!" and "SantaLand Diaries"
previously appeared in *Barrel Fever*; "Dinah, the Christmas Whore" previously
appeared in *Naked*; "Jesus Shaves" previously appeared in slightly different form
in *Me Talk Pretty One Day*; "Us and Them," "Let It Snow," and "Six to Eight
Black Men" previously appeared in *Dress Your Family in Corduroy and Denim*;
and "The Monster Mash" previously appeared in *When You Are Engulfed in
Flames*.

Little, Brown and Company is a division of Hachette Book Group, Inc.
The Little, Brown name and logo are trademarks of Hachette Book Group, Inc.

ISBN 978-0-316-03590-3
LCCN 2008925927

10 9 8 7 6 5 4 3 2 1

RRD-IN

Printed in the United States of America

To Ira Glass

Contents

Holidays on Ice

SantaLand Diaries

I was in a coffee shop looking through the want ads when I read, "Macy's Herald Square, the largest store in the world, has big opportunities for outgoing, fun-loving people of all shapes and sizes who want more than just a holiday job! Working as an elf in Macy's SantaLand means being at the center of the excitement. . . ."

I circled the ad and then I laughed out loud at the thought of it. The man seated next to me turned on his stool, checking to see if I was a lunatic. I continued to laugh, quietly. Yesterday I applied for a job at UPS. They are hiring drivers' helpers for the upcoming Christmas season and I went to their headquarters filled with hope. In line with three hundred other men and women my hope diminished. During the brief interview I was asked why I wanted to work for UPS and I answered that I wanted to work for UPS because I like the brown uniforms. What did they expect me to say?

"I'd like to work for UPS because, in my opinion, it's an opportunity to showcase my substantial leadership skills in one of the finest private delivery companies this country has seen since the Pony Express!"

I said I liked the uniforms and the UPS interviewer turned my application facedown on his desk and said, "Give me a break."

I came home this afternoon and checked the machine for a message from UPS but the only message I got was from the company that holds my student loan, Sallie Mae. Sallie Mae sounds like a naive and barefoot hillbilly girl but in fact they are a ruthless and aggressive conglomeration of bullies located in a tall brick building somewhere in Kansas. I picture it to be the tallest building in that state and I have decided they hire their employees straight out of prison. It scares me.

The woman at Macy's asked, "Would you be interested in full-time elf or evening and weekend elf?"

I said, "Full-time elf."

I have an appointment next Wednesday at noon.

I am a thirty-three-year-old man applying for a job as an elf.

I often see people on the streets dressed as objects and handing out leaflets. I tend to avoid leaflets but it breaks my heart to see a grown man dressed as a taco. So, if there is a costume involved, I tend not only to accept the leaflet, but to accept it graciously, saying, "Thank you so much," and thinking, *You poor, pathetic son of a bitch. I don't know what you have but I hope I never catch it.* This afternoon on Lexington Avenue I accepted a leaflet from a man dressed as a camcorder. Hot dogs, peanuts, tacos, video cameras, these things make me sad because they don't fit in on the streets. In a parade, maybe, but not on the streets. I figure that at least as an elf I will have a place; I'll be in Santa's Village with all the other elves. We will reside in a fluffy wonderland surrounded by candy canes and gingerbread shacks. It won't be quite as sad as standing on some street corner dressed as a french fry.

        I am trying to look on the bright side. I arrived in New York three weeks ago with high hopes, hopes that have been challenged. In my imagination I'd go straight from Penn Station to the offices of "One Life to Live," where I would drop off my bags and spruce up before heading off for drinks with Cord Roberts and Victoria Buchannon, the show's greatest stars. We'd sit in a plush booth at a tony cocktail lounge where my new celebrity friends would lift their frosty glasses in my direction and say, "A toast to David Sedaris, the best writer this show has ever had!!!"

I'd say, "You guys, cut it out." It was my plan to act modest.

People at surrounding tables would stare at us, whispering, "Isn't that . . . ? Isn't that . . . ?"

I might be distracted by their enthusiasm and Victoria Buchannon would lay her hand over mine and tell me that I'd better get used to being the center of attention.

But instead I am applying for a job as an elf. Even worse than applying is the very real possibility that I will not be hired, that I couldn't even find work as an elf. That's when you know you're a failure.

This afternoon I sat in the eighth-floor SantaLand office and was told, "Congratulations, Mr. Sedaris. You are an elf."

In order to become an elf I filled out ten pages' worth of forms, took a multiple choice personality test, underwent two interviews, and submitted urine for a drug test. The first interview was general, designed to eliminate the obvious sociopaths. During the second interview we were asked why we wanted to be elves. This is always a problem question. I listened as the woman ahead of me, a former waitress, answered the question, saying, "I really want to be an elf? Because I think it's about acting? And before this I worked in a restaurant? Which was run by this really wonderful woman who had a dream to open a restaurant? And it made me realize that it's really really . . . important to have a . . . dream?"

Everything this woman said, every phrase and sentence, was punctuated with a question mark and the interviewer never raised an eyebrow.

When it was my turn I explained that I wanted to be an elf because it was one of the most frightening career opportunities I had ever come across. The interviewer raised her face from my application and said, "And . . . ?"

I'm certain that I failed my drug test. My urine had roaches and stems floating in it, but still they hired me because I am short, five feet five inches. Almost everyone they hired is short. One is a dwarf. After the second interview I was brought to the manager's office, where I was shown a floor plan. On a busy day twenty-two thousand people come to visit Santa, and I was told that it is an elf's lot to remain merry in the face of torment and adversity. I promised to keep that in mind.

I spent my eight-hour day with fifty elves and one perky, well-meaning instructor in an enormous Macy's class-room, the walls of which were lined with NCR 2152's. A 2152, I have come to understand, is a cash register. The class was broken up into study groups and given assignments. My group included several returning elves and a few experienced cashiers who tried helping me by saying things like, "Don't you even know your per-sonal ID code? Jesus, I had mine memorized by ten o'clock."

Everything about the cash register intimidates me. Each proce-dure involves a series of codes: separate numbers for cash, checks, and each type of credit card. The term *Void* has gained prominence as the filthiest four-letter word in my vocabulary. Voids are a night-mare of paperwork and coded numbers, everything produced in triplicate and initialed by the employee and his supervisor.

Leaving the building tonight I could not shake the mental pic-ture of myself being stoned to death by restless, angry customers, their nerves shattered by my complete lack of skill. I tell myself that I will simply pry open my register and accept anything they want to give me — beads, cash, watches, whatever. I'll negotiate and swap. I'll stomp their credit cards through the masher, write "Nice Knowing You!" along the bottom of the slip, and leave it at that.

All we sell in SantaLand are photos. People sit upon Santa's lap and pose for a picture. The Photo Elf hands them a slip of paper with a number printed along the top. The form is filled out by another elf and the picture arrives by mail weeks later. So really, all we sell is the idea of a picture. One idea costs nine dollars, three ideas cost eighteen.

My worst nightmare involves twenty-two thousand people a day standing before my register. I won't always be a cashier, just once in a while. The worst part is that after I have accumulated three hundred dollars I have to remove two hundred, fill out half a dozen forms, and run the envelope of cash to the drop in the China Department or to the vault on the balcony above the first floor. I am not allowed to change my clothes beforehand. I have to go dressed as an elf. An elf in SantaLand is one thing, an elf in Sportswear is something else altogether.

This afternoon we were given presentations and speeches in a windowless conference room crowded with desks and plastic chairs. We were told that during the second week of December, SantaLand is host to "Operation Special

DAVID SEDARIS

Children," at which time poor children receive free gifts donated by the store. There is another morning set aside for terribly sick and deformed children. On that day it is an elf's job to greet the child at the Magic Tree and jog back to the house to brace our Santa.

"The next one is missing a nose," or "Crystal has third-degree burns covering 90 percent of her body."

Missing a nose. With these children Santa has to be careful not to ask, "And what would *you* like for Christmas?"

We were given a lecture by the chief of security, who told us that Macy's Herald Square suffers millions of dollars' worth of employee theft per year. As a result the store treats its employees the way one might treat a felon with a long criminal record. Cash rewards are offered for turning people in and our bags are searched every time we leave the store. We were shown videotapes in which supposed former employees hang their head and rue the day they ever thought to steal that leather jacket. The actors faced the camera to explain how their arrests had ruined their friendships, family life, and, ultimately, their future.

One fellow stared at his hands and sighed, "There's no way I'm going to be admitted into law school. Not now. Not after what I've done. Nope, no way." He paused and shook his head of the unpleasant memory. "Oh, man, not after this. No way."

A lonely, reflective girl sat in a coffee shop, considered her empty cup, and moaned, "I remember going out after work with all my Macy's friends. God, those were good times. I loved those people." She stared off into space for a few moments before continuing, "Well, needless to say, those friends aren't calling anymore. This time I've *really* messed up. Why did I do it? Why?"

Macy's has two jail cells on the balcony floor and it apprehends three thousand shoplifters a year. We were told to keep an eye out for pickpockets in SantaLand.

Interpreters for the deaf came and taught us to sign, "MERRY CHRISTMAS! I AM SANTA'S HELPER." They told us to speak as we sign and to use bold, clear voices and bright facial expressions. They taught us to say, "YOU ARE A VERY PRETTY BOY/GIRL! I LOVE YOU! DO YOU WANT A SURPRISE?"

My sister Amy lives above a deaf girl and has learned quite a bit of sign language. She taught some to me and so now I am able to say, "SANTA HAS A TUMOR IN HIS HEAD THE SIZE OF AN OLIVE. MAYBE IT WILL GO AWAY TOMORROW BUT I DON'T THINK SO."

This morning we were lectured by the Santa-Land managers and presented with a Xeroxed booklet of regulations titled "The Elfin Guide." Most of the managers are former elves who have worked their way up the candy-cane ladder but retain vivid memories of their days in uniform. They closed the meeting saying, "I want you to remember that even if you are assigned Photo Elf on a busy weekend, YOU ARE NOT SANTA'S SLAVE."

DAVID SEDARIS

In the afternoon we were given a tour of SantaLand, which really is something. It's beautiful, a real wonderland, with ten thousand sparkling lights, false snow, train sets, bridges, decorated trees, mechanical penguins and bears, and really tall candy canes. One enters and travels through a maze, a path which takes you from one festive environment to another. The path ends at the Magic Tree. The Tree is supposed to resemble a complex system of roots, but looks instead like a scale model of the human intestinal tract. Once you pass the Magic Tree, the light dims and an elf guides you to Santa's house. The houses are cozy and intimate, laden with toys. You exit Santa's house and are met with a line of cash registers.

We traveled the path a second time and were given the code names for various posts, such as "The Vomit Corner," a mirrored wall near the Magic Tree, where nauseous children tend to surrender the contents of their stomachs. When someone vomits, the nearest elf is supposed to yell "VAMOOSE," which is the name of the janitorial product used by the store. We were taken to the "Oh, My God, Corner," a position near the escalator. People arriving see the long line and say "Oh, my God!" and it is an elf's job to calm them down and explain that it will take no longer than an hour to see Santa.

On any given day you can be an Entrance Elf, a Water Cooler Elf, a Bridge Elf, Train Elf, Maze Elf, Island Elf, Magic Window Elf, Emergency Exit Elf, Counter Elf, Magic Tree Elf, Pointer Elf, Santa Elf, Photo Elf, Usher Elf, Cash Register Elf, Runner Elf, or

Exit Elf. We were given a demonstration of the various positions in action, performed by returning elves who were so animated and relentlessly cheerful that it embarrassed me to walk past them. I don't know that I could look someone in the eye and exclaim, "Oh, my goodness, I think I see Santa!" or "Can you close your eyes and make a very special Christmas wish!" Everything these elves said had an exclamation point at the end of it!!! It makes one's mouth hurt to speak with such forced merriment. I feel cornered when someone talks to me this way. Doesn't everyone? I prefer being frank with children. I'm more likely to say, "You must be exhausted," or "I know a lot of people who would kill for that little waistline of yours."

I am afraid I won't be able to provide the grinding enthusiasm Santa is asking for. I think I'll be a low-key sort of an elf.

Today was elf dress rehearsal. The lockers and dressing rooms are located on the eighth floor, directly behind SantaLand. Elves have gotten to know one another over the past four days of training but once we took off our clothes and put on the uniforms everything changed.

The woman in charge of costuming assigned us our outfits and gave us a lecture on keeping things clean. She held up a calendar and said, "Ladies, you know what this is. Use it. I have scraped enough blood out from the crotches of elf knickers to last me the rest of my life. And don't tell me, 'I don't wear underpants,

I'm a dancer.' You're not a dancer. If you were a real dancer you wouldn't be here. You're an elf and you're going to wear panties like an elf."

My costume is green. I wear green velvet knickers, a yellow turtleneck, a forest-green velvet smock, and a perky stocking cap decorated with spangles. This is my work uniform.

My elf name is Crumpet. We were allowed to choose our own names and given permission to change them according to our outlook on the snowy world.

Today was the official opening day of Santa-Land and I worked as a Magic Window Elf, a Santa Elf, and an Usher Elf. The Magic Window is located in the adult "Quick Peep" line. My job was to say, "Step on the Magic Star and look through the window, and you can see Santa!" I was at the Magic Window for fifteen minutes before a man approached me and said, "You look so fucking stupid."

I have to admit that he had a point. But still, I wanted to say that at least I get paid to look stupid, that he gives it away for free. But I can't say things like that because I'm supposed to be merry.

So instead I said, "Thank you!"

"Thank you!" as if I had misunderstood and thought he had said, "You look terrific."

"Thank you!"

He was a brawny wise guy wearing a vinyl jacket and carrying a bag from Radio Shack. I should have said, real loud, "Sorry, man, I don't date other guys."

Two New Jersey families came together to see Santa. Two loud, ugly husbands with two wives and four children between them. The children gathered around Santa and had their picture taken. When Santa asked the ten-year-old boy what he wanted for Christmas, his father shouted, "A WOMAN! GET HIM A WOMAN, SANTA!" These men were very rude and irritating, constantly laughing and jostling one another. The two women sat on Santa's lap and had their pictures taken and each asked Santa for a KitchenAid brand dishwasher and a decent winter coat. Then the husbands sat on Santa's lap and, when asked what he wanted for Christmas, one of the men yelled, "I WANT A BROAD WITH BIG TITS." The man's small-breasted wife crossed her arms over her chest, looked at the floor, and gritted her teeth. The man's son tried to laugh.

Again this morning I got stuck at the Magic Window, which is really boring. I'm supposed to stand around and say, "Step on the Magic Star and you can see Santa!" I said that for a while and then I started saying, "Step on the Magic Star and you can see Cher!"

And people got excited. So I said, "Step on the Magic Star and you can see Mike Tyson!"

Some people in the other line, the line to sit on Santa's lap, got excited and cut through the gates so that they could stand on my Magic Star. Then they got angry when they looked through the Magic Window and saw Santa rather than Cher or Mike Tyson. What did they honestly expect? Is Cher so hard up for money that she'd agree to stand behind a two-way mirror at Macy's?

The angry people must have said something to management because I was taken off the Magic Star and sent to Elf Island, which is really boring as all you do is stand around and act merry. At noon a huge crowd of retarded people came to visit Santa and passed me on my little island. These people were profoundly retarded. They were rolling their eyes and wagging their tongues and staggering toward Santa. It was a large group of retarded people and after watching them for a few minutes I could not begin to guess where the retarded people ended and the regular New Yorkers began.

Everyone looks retarded once you set your mind to it.

This evening I was sent to be a Photo Elf, a job I enjoyed the first few times. The camera is hidden in the fireplace and I take the picture by pressing a button at the end of a cord. The pictures arrive by mail weeks later and there is no way an elf can be identified and held accountable but still, you want to make it a good picture.

During our training we were shown photographs that had gone wrong, blurred frenzies of an elf's waving arm, a picture blocked by a stuffed animal, the yawning Santa. After every photograph an elf must remove the numbered form that appears at the bottom of the picture. A lazy or stupid elf could ruin an entire roll of film, causing eager families to pay for and later receive photographs of complete, beaming strangers.

Taking someone's picture tells you an awful lot, *awful* being the operative word. Having the parents in the room tends to make it even worse. It is the SantaLand policy to take a picture of every child, which the parent can either order or refuse. People are allowed to bring their own cameras, video recorders, whatever. It is the multimedia groups that exhaust me. These are parents bent over with equipment, relentless in their quest for documentation.

I see them in the Maze with their video cameras instructing their children to act surprised. "Monica, baby, look at the train set and look back at me. No, look at *me*. Now wave. That's right, wave hard."

The parents hold up the line and it is a Maze Elf's job to hurry them along.

"Excuse me, sir, I'm sorry but we're sort of busy today and I'd appreciate it if you could maybe wrap this up. There are quite a few people behind you."

The parent then asks you to stand beside the child and wave. I do so. I stand beside a child and wave to the video camera, wondering where I will wind up. I picture myself on the television set in a paneled room in Wapahanset or Easternmost Meadows. I imagine the family fighting over command of the remote control, hitting the fast-forward button. The child's wave becomes a rapid salute. I enter the picture and everyone in the room entertains the same thought: "What's that asshole doing on our Christmas Memory tape?"

The moment these people are waiting for is the encounter with Santa. As a Photo Elf I watch them enter the room and take control.

"All right, Ellen, I want you and Marcus to stand in front of Santa and when I say, 'now,' I want you to get onto his lap. Look at me now. Look at Daddy until I tell you to look at Santa."

He will address his wife, who is working the still camera, and she will crouch low to the ground with her light meter and a Nikon with many attachments. It is heavy and the veins in her arms stand out.

Then there are the multimedia families in groups, who say, "All right, now let's get a shot of Anthony, Damascus, Theresa, Doug, Amy, Paul, *and* Vanity — can we squeeze them all together? Santa, how about you let Doug sit on your shoulders, can we do that?"

During these visits the children are rarely allowed to discuss their desires with Santa. They are too busy being art-directed by the parents.

"Vanity and Damascus, look over here, no, look *here*."

"Santa, can you put your arm around Amy and shake hands with Paul at the same time?"

"That's good. That's nice."

I have seen parents sit their child upon Santa's lap and immediately proceed to groom: combing hair, arranging a hemline, straightening a necktie. I saw a parent spray their child's hair, Santa treated as though he were a false prop made of cement, turning his head and wincing as the hair spray stung his eyes.

Young children, ages two to four, tend to be frightened of Santa. They have no interest in having their pictures taken because they don't know what a picture is. They're not vain, they're babies. They are babies and they act accordingly — they cry. A Photo Elf understands that, once a child starts crying, it's over. They start crying in Santa's house and they don't stop until they are at least ten blocks away.

When the child starts crying, Santa will offer comfort for a moment or two before saying, "Maybe we'll try again next year."

The parents had planned to send the photos to relatives and place them in scrapbooks. They waited in line for over an hour and are not about to give up so easily. Tonight I saw a woman slap and shake her sobbing daughter, yelling, "Goddamn it, Rachel, get on that man's lap and smile or I'll give you something to cry about."

I often take photographs of crying children. Even more

grotesque is taking a picture of a crying child with a false grimace. It's not a smile so much as the forced shape of a smile. Oddly, it pleases the parents.

"Good girl, Rachel. Now, let's get the hell out of here. Your mother has a headache that won't quit until you're twenty-one."

At least a third of Santa's visitors are adults: couples, and a surprising number of men and women alone. Most of the single people don't want to sit on Santa's lap; they just stop by to shake his hand and wish him luck. Often the single adults are foreigners who just happened to be shopping at Macy's and got bullied into the Maze by the Entrance Elf, whose job it is to hustle people in. One moment the foreigner is looking at china, and the next thing he knows he is standing at the Magic Tree, where an elf holding a palm-sized counter is asking how many in his party are here to see Santa.

"How many in your party?"

The foreigner answers, "Yes."

"How many in your party is not a yes or no question."

"Yes."

Then a Santa Elf leads the way to a house where the confused and exhausted visitor addresses a bearded man in a red suit, and says, "Yes, OK. Today I am good." He shakes Santa's hand and runs, shaken, for the back door.

This afternoon a man came to visit Santa, a sloppy, good-looking man in his mid-forties. I thought he was another confused European, so I reassured him that many adults come to visit Santa, everyone is welcome. An hour later, I noticed the same man, back again to fellowship with Santa. I asked what he and Santa talk about, and in a cracked and puny voice he answered, "Toys. All the toys."

I noticed a dent in the left side of his forehead. You could place an acorn in a dent like this. He waited in line and returned to visit a third time. On his final visit he got so excited he peed on Santa's lap.

So far in SantaLand, I have seen Simone from "General Hospital," Shawn from "All My Children," Walter Cronkite, and Phil Collins. Last year one of the elves was suspended after asking Goldie Hawn to autograph her hand. We have been instructed to leave the stars alone.

Walter Cronkite was very tall, and I probably wouldn't have recognized him unless someone had pointed him out to me. Phil Collins was small and well-groomed. He arrived with his daughter and an entourage of three. I don't care about Phil Collins one way or the other but I saw some people who might and I felt it was my duty to tap them on the shoulder and say, "Look, there's Phil Collins!"

Many of Santa's visitors are from out of town and welcome the opportunity to view a celebrity, as it rounds out their New York experience. I'd point out Phil Collins and people would literally squeal with delight. Seeing as it is my job to make people happy, I didn't have any problem with it. Phil Collins wandered through the Maze, videotaping everything with his camcorder and enjoying himself. Once he entered the Magic Tree, he was no longer visible to the Maze audience, so I began telling people that if they left immediately and took a right at the end of the hall, they could probably catch up with Phil Collins after his visit with Santa. So they did. People left. When Phil Collins walked out of SantaLand, there was a crowd of twenty people waiting for autographs. When the managers came looking for the big mouth, I said, "Phil Collins, who's he?"

I spent a few hours in the Maze with Puff, a young elf from Brooklyn. We were standing near the Lollipop Forest when we realized that *Santa* is an anagram of *Satan*. Father Christmas or the Devil — so close but yet so far. We imagined a SatanLand where visitors would wade through steaming pools of human blood and feces before arriving at the Gates of Hell, where a hideous imp in a singed velvet costume would take them by the hand and lead them toward Satan. Once we thought of it we couldn't get it out of our minds. Overhearing the customers we would substitute the word *Satan* for the word *Santa*.

"What do you think, Michael? Do you think Macy's has the real Satan?"

"Don't forget to thank Satan for the Baby Alive he gave you last year."

"I love Satan."

"Who doesn't? Everyone loves Satan."

I would rather drive upholstery tacks into my gums than work as the Usher Elf. The Usher stands outside Santa's exit door and fills out the photo forms. While I enjoy trying to guess where people are from, I hate listening to couples bicker over how many copies they want.

It was interesting the first time I did it, but not anymore. While the parents make up their minds, the Usher has to prevent the excited children from entering Santa's back door to call out the names of three or four toys they had neglected to request earlier.

When things are slow, an Usher pokes in his head and watches Santa with his visitors. This afternoon we were slow and I watched a forty-year-old woman and her ancient mother step in to converse with Santa. The daughter wore a short pink dress, decorated with lace — the type of dress that a child might wear. Her hair was trained into pigtails and she wore ruffled socks and patent leather shoes. This forty-year-old girl ran to Santa and embraced him, driving rouge into his beard. She spoke in a baby voice and then lowered it to a whisper. When they left I asked if they wanted to purchase the photo and the biggest little girl in the world whispered something in her mother's ear and then she skipped away. She skipped. I watched her try and commune with the youngsters standing around the register until her mother pulled her away.

This morning I spent some time at the Magic Window with Sleighbell, an entertainer who is in the process of making a music video with her all-girl singing group. We talked about one thing and another, and she told me that she has appeared on a few television shows, mainly soap operas. I asked if she has ever done "One Life to Live," and she said, yes, she had a bit part as a flamenco dancer a few years ago when Cord and Tina remarried and traveled to Madrid for their honeymoon.

Suddenly I remembered Sleighbell perfectly. On that episode she wore a red lace dress and stomped upon a shiny nightclub floor until Spain's greatest bullfighter entered, challenging Cord to a duel. Sleighbell intervened. She stopped dancing and said to Cord, "Don't do it, Señor. Yoot be a fool to fight weeth Spain's greatest boolfighter!"

Sleighbell told me that the honeymoon was filmed here in the New York studio. That surprised me as I really thought it was shot in Spain. She told me that the dancing scene was shot in the late morning and afterwards there was a break for lunch. She took her lunch in the studio cafeteria and was holding her tray, when Tina waved her over to her table. Sleighbell had lunch with Tina! She said that Tina was very sweet and talked about her love for Smokey

Robinson. I had read that Tina had driven a wedge between Smokey and his wife, but it was thrilling to hear it from someone who had the facts.

Later in the day I was put on the cash register where Andrea, one of the managers, told me that her friend Caroline was the person responsible for casting on "One Life to Live." It was Caroline who replaced the old Tina with the new Tina. I loved the old Tina and will accept no substitutes, but I told Andrea that I liked the new Tina a lot, and she said, "I'll pass that along to Caroline. She'll be happy to hear it!" We were talking when Mitchell, another manager, got involved and said that he'd been on "One Life to Live" seven times. He played Clint's lawyer five years ago when the entire Buchannon family was on trial for the murder of Mitch Laurence. Mitchell knows Victoria Buchannon personally and said that she's just as sweet and caring in real life as she is on the show.

"She's basically playing herself, except for the multiple personality disorder," he said, pausing to verify a check on another elf's register. He asked the customer for another form of ID, and while the woman cursed and fished through her purse, Mitchell told me that Clint tends to keep to himself but that Bo and Asa are a lot of fun.

I can't believe I'm hearing these things. I know people who have sat around with Tina, Cord, Nicki, Asa, and Clint. I'm getting closer, I can feel it.

This evening I was working as a Counter Elf at the Magic Tree when I saw a woman unzip her son's fly, release his penis, and instruct him to pee into a bank of artificial snow. He was a young child, four or five years old, and he did it, he peed. Urine dripped from the branches of artificial trees and puddled on the floor.

Tonight a man proposed to his girlfriend in one of the Santa houses. When Santa asked the man what he wanted for Christmas, he pulled a ring out of his pocket and said he wanted this woman to be his wife. Santa congratulated them both and the Photo Elf got choked up and started crying.

A spotted child visited Santa, climbed up on his lap, and expressed a wish to recover from chicken pox. Santa leapt up.

I've met elves from all walks of life. Most of them are show business people, actors and dancers, but a surprising number of them held real jobs at advertising agencies and brokerage firms before the recession hit. Bless their hearts, these people never imagined there was a velvet costume waiting in their future. They're the really bitter elves. Many of the elves are young, high school and college students. They're young and cute and one of the job perks is that I get to see them in their underpants. The changing rooms are located in the employee bathrooms behind SantaLand. The men's bathroom is small and the toilets often flood, so we are forced to stand on an island of newspapers in order to keep our socks dry. The Santas have a nice dressing room across the hall, but you don't want to see a Santa undress. Quite a few elves have taken to changing clothes in the hallway, beside their lockers. These elves tend to wear bathing suits underneath their costumes — jams, I believe they are called. I don't like jams.

The overall cutest elf is a fellow from Queens named Snowball. Snowball tends to ham it up with the children, sometimes literally tumbling down the path to Santa's house. I tend to frown on that sort of behavior but Snowball is hands down adorable — you want to put him in your pocket. Yesterday we worked together as Santa Elves and I became excited when he started saying things like, "I'd follow *you* to Santa's house any day, Crumpet."

It made me dizzy, this flirtation.

By mid-afternoon I was running into walls. At the end of our shift we were in the bathroom, changing clothes, when suddenly we were surrounded by three Santas and five other elves — all of them were guys that Snowball had been flirting with.

Snowball just leads elves on, elves and Santas. He is playing a dangerous game.

DAVID SEDARIS

This afternoon I was stuck being Photo Elf with Santa Santa. I don't know his real name; no one does. During most days, there is a slow period when you sit around the house and talk to your Santa. Most of them are nice guys and we sit around and laugh, but Santa Santa takes himself a bit too seriously. I asked him where he lives, Brooklyn or Manhattan, and he said, "Why, I live at the North Pole with Mrs. Claus!" I asked what he does the rest of the year and he said, "I make toys for all of the children."

I said, "Yes, but what do you do for money?"

"Santa doesn't need money," he said.

Santa Santa sits and waves and jingles his bell sash when no one is there. He actually recited "The Night Before Christmas," and it was just the two of us in the house, no children. Just us. What do you do with a nut like that?

He says, "Oh, Little Elf, Little Elf, straighten up those mantel toys for Santa." I reminded him that I have a name, Crumpet, and then I straightened up the stuffed animals.

"Oh, Little Elf, Little Elf, bring Santa a throat lozenge." So I brought him a lozenge.

Santa Santa has an elaborate little act for the children. He'll talk to them and give a hearty chuckle and ring his bells and then he asks them to name their favorite Christmas carol. Most of them say "Rudolph, the Red-Nosed Reindeer." Santa Santa then asks if they will sing it for him. The children are shy and don't want to sing out loud, so Santa Santa says, "Oh, Little Elf, Little Elf! Help young Brenda to sing that favorite carol of hers." Then I have to stand there and sing "Rudolph, the Red-Nosed Reindeer," which I hate. Half the time young Brenda's parents are my age and that certainly doesn't help matters much.

This afternoon I worked as an Exit Elf, telling people in a loud voice, "THIS WAY OUT OF SANTALAND." A woman was standing at one of the cash registers paying for her idea of a picture, while her son lay beneath her kicking and heaving, having a tantrum.

The woman said, "Riley, if you don't start behaving yourself, Santa's not going to bring you *any* of those toys you asked for."

The child said, "He is too going to bring me toys, liar, he already told me."

The woman grabbed my arm and said, "You there, Elf, tell Riley here that if he doesn't start behaving immediately, then Santa's going to change his mind and bring him coal for Christmas."

I said that Santa no longer traffics in coal. Instead, if you're bad he comes to your house and steals things. I told Riley that if he didn't behave himself, Santa was going to take away his TV and all his electrical appliances and leave him in the dark. "All your appliances, including the refrigerator. Your food is going to spoil and smell bad. It's going to be so cold and dark where you are. Man, Riley, are you ever going to suffer. You're going to wish you never heard the name Santa."

The woman got a worried look on her face and said, "All right, that's enough."

I said, "He's going to take your car and your furniture and all the towels and blankets and leave you with nothing."

The mother said, "No, that's enough, really."

I spend all day lying to people, saying, "You look so pretty," and, "Santa can't wait to visit with you. You're all he talks about. It's just not Christmas without you. You're Santa's favorite person in the entire tri-state area." Sometimes I lay it on real thick: "Aren't you the Princess of Rongovia? Santa said a beautiful princess was coming here to visit him. He said she would be wearing a red dress and that she was very pretty, but not stuck up or two-faced. That's you, isn't it?" I lay it on and the parents mouth the words "Thank you" and "Good job."

To one child I said, "You're a model, aren't you?" The girl was maybe six years old and said, "Yes, I model, but I also act. I just got a second callback for a Fisher-Price commercial." The girl's mother said, "You may recognize Katelyn from the 'My First Sony' campaign. She's on the box." I said yes, of course.

All I do is lie, and that has made me immune to compliments.

Lately I am feeling trollish and have changed my elf name from Crumpet to Blisters. Blisters — I think it's cute.

Today a child told Santa Ken that he wanted his dead father back *and* a complete set of Teenage Mutant Ninja Turtles. Everyone wants those Turtles.

Last year a woman decided she wanted a picture of her cat sitting on Santa's lap, so she smuggled it into Macy's in a duffel bag. The cat sat on Santa's lap for five seconds before it shot out the door, and it took six elves forty-five minutes before they found it in the kitchen of the employee cafeteria.

A child came to Santa this morning and his mother said, "All right, Jason. Tell Santa what you want. Tell him what you want."

Jason said, "I . . . want . . . Prokton and . . . Gamble to . . . stop animal testing."

The mother said, "Procter, Jason, that's Procter and Gamble. And what do they do to animals? Do they torture animals, Jason? Is that what they do?"

Jason said, Yes, they torture. He was probably six years old.

This week my least favorite elf is a guy from Florida whom I call "The Walrus." The Walrus has a handlebar mustache, no chin, and a neck the size of my waist. In the dressing room he confesses to being "a bit of a ladies' man."

The Walrus acts as though SantaLand were a singles bar. It is embarrassing to work with him. We'll be together at the Magic Window, where he pulls women aside, places his arm around their shoulders, and says, "I know you're not going to ask Santa for good looks. You've already got those, pretty lady. Yes, indeed, you've got those in spades."

In his mind the women are charmed, dizzy with his attention.

I pull him aside and say, "That was a *mother* you just did that to, a married woman with three children."

He says, "I didn't see any ring." Then he turns to the next available woman and whistles. "Santa's married but I'm not. Hey, pretty lady, I've got plenty of room on my knee."

I Photo Elfed all day for a variety of Santas and it struck me that many of the parents don't allow their children to speak at all. A child sits upon Santa's lap and the parents say, "All right now, Amber, tell Santa what you want. Tell him you want a Baby Alive and My Pretty Ballerina and that winter coat you saw in the catalog."

The parents name the gifts they have already bought. They don't want to hear the word "pony," or "television set," so they talk through the entire visit, placing words in the child's mouth. When the child hops off the lap, the parents address their children, each and every time, with, "What do you say to Santa?"

The child says, "Thank you, Santa."

It is sad because you would like to believe that everyone is unique and then they disappoint you every time by being exactly the same, asking for the same things, reciting the exact same lines as though they have been handed a script.

All of the adults ask for a Gold Card or a BMW and they rock with laughter, thinking they are the first person brazen enough to request such pleasures.

Santa says, "I'll see what I can do."

Couples over the age of fifty all say, "I don't want to sit on your lap, Santa, I'm afraid I might break it!"

How do you break a lap? How did so many people get the idea to say the exact same thing?

I went to a store on the Upper West Side. This store is like a Museum of Natural History where everything is for sale: every taxidermic or skeletal animal that roams the earth is represented in this shop and, because of that, it is popular. I went with my brother last weekend. Near the cash register was a bowl of glass eyes and a sign reading "DO NOT HOLD THESE GLASS EYES UP AGAINST YOUR OWN EYES: THE ROUGH STEM CAN CAUSE INJURY."

I talked to the fellow behind the counter and he said, "It's the same thing every time. First they hold up the eyes and then they go for the horns. I'm sick of it."

It disturbed me that, until I saw the sign, my first impulse was to hold those eyes up to my own. I thought it might be a laugh riot.

All of us take pride and pleasure in the fact that we are unique, but I'm afraid that when all is said and done the police are right: it all comes down to fingerprints.

There was a big "Sesame Street Live" extravaganza over at Madison Square Garden, so thousands of people decided to make a day of it and go straight from Sesame Street to Santa. We were packed today, absolutely packed, and everyone was cranky. Once the line gets long we break it up into four different lines because anyone in their right mind would leave if they knew it would take over two hours to see Santa. Two hours — you could see a movie in two hours. Standing in a two-hour line makes people worry that they're not living in a democratic nation. People stand in line for two hours and they go over the edge. I was sent into the hallway to direct the second phase of the line. The hallway was packed with people, and all of them seemed to stop me with a question: which way to the down escalator, which way to the elevator, the Patio Restaurant, gift wrap, the women's rest room, Trim-A-Tree. There was a line for Santa and a line for the women's bathroom, and one woman, after asking me a dozen questions already, asked, "Which is the line for the women's bathroom?" I shouted that I thought it was the line with all the women in it.

She said, "I'm going to have you fired."

I had two people say that to me today, "I'm going to have you fired." Go ahead, be my guest. I'm wearing a green velvet costume; it doesn't get any worse than this. Who do these people think they are?

"I'm going to have you fired!" and I wanted to lean over and say, "I'm going to have you killed."

In the Maze, on the way to Santa's house, you pass spectacles — train sets, dancing bears, the candy-cane forest, and the penguins. The penguins are set in their own icy wonderland. They were built years ago and they frolic mechanically. They stand outside their igloo and sled and skate and fry fish in a pan. For some reason people feel compelled to throw coins into the penguin display. I can't figure it out for the life of me — they don't throw money at the tree of gifts or the mechanical elves, or the mailbox of letters, but they empty their pockets for the penguins. I asked what happens to that money, and a manager told me that it's collected for charity, but I don't think so. Elves take the quarters for the pay phone, housekeeping takes the dimes, and I've seen visitors, those that aren't throwing money, I've seen them scooping it up as fast as they can.

I was working the Exit today. I'm supposed to say, "This way *out* of SantaLand," but I can't bring myself to say it as it seems like I'm rushing people. They wait an hour to see Santa, they're hit up for photo money, and then someone's hustling them out. I say,

"This way *out* of SantaLand if you've decided maybe it's time for you to go home."

"You can exit this way if you feel like it."

We're also supposed to encourage people to wait outside while the parent with money is paying for a picture. "If you're waiting for someone to purchase a photo, wait *outside* the double doors."

I say, "If you're waiting for someone to purchase a picture, you might want to wait *outside* the double doors where it is pleasant and the light is more flattering."

I had a group of kids waiting this afternoon, waiting for their mom to pay for pictures, and this kid reached into his pocket and threw a nickel at me. He was maybe twelve years old, jaded in regard to Santa, and he threw his nickel and it hit my chest and fell to the floor. I picked it up, cleared my throat, and handed it back to him. He threw it again. Like I was a penguin. So I handed it back and he threw it higher, hitting me in the neck. I picked up the nickel and turned to another child and said, "Here, you dropped this." He examined the coin, put it in his pocket, and left.

Yesterday was my day off, and the afflicted came to visit Santa. I Photo Elfed for Santa Ira this afternoon, and he told me all about it. These were severely handicapped children who arrived on stretchers and in wheelchairs. Santa couldn't put them on his lap, and often he could not understand them when they voiced their requests. Still, though, he made it a point to grab each child's hand and ask what they wanted for Christmas. He did this until he came to a child who had no hands. This made him self-conscious, so he started placing a hand on the child's knee until he came to a child with no legs. After that he decided to simply nod his head and chuckle.

I got stuck with Santa Santa again this afternoon and had to sing and fetch for three hours. Late in the afternoon, a child said she didn't know what her favorite Christmas carol was. Santa said, " 'Rudolph'? 'Jingle Bells'? 'White Christmas'? 'Here Comes Santa Claus'? 'Away in a Manger'? 'Silent Night'?"

The girl agreed to "Away in a Manger," but didn't want to sing it because she didn't know the words.

Santa Santa said, "Oh, Little Elf, Little Elf, come sing 'Away in a Manger' for us."

It didn't seem fair that I should have to solo, so I told him I didn't know the words.

Santa Santa said, "Of course you know the words. Come now, sing!"

So I sang it the way Billie Holliday might have sung it if she'd put out a Christmas album. "Away in a manger, no crib for a bed, the little Lord, Jesus, lay down his sweet head."

Santa Santa did not allow me to finish.

This afternoon we set a record by scooting fourteen hundred people through SantaLand in the course of an hour. Most of them were school groups in clots of thirty or more. My Santa would address them, saying, "All right, I'm going to count to three, and on three I want you all to yell what you want and I need you to say it as loud as you can."

Then he would count to three and the noise was magnificent. Santa would cover his ears and say, "Okay, then — one by one I want you to tell me what you're planning to leave Santa on Christmas Eve."

He would go around the room and children would name different sorts of cookies, and he would say, "What about sandwiches? What if Santa should want something more substantial than a cookie?"

Santa's thrust this afternoon was the boredom of his nine-year relationship. He would wave the children good-bye and then turn to me, saying, "I want an affair, goddamn it — just a little one, just something to get me through the next four or five years."

Some of these children, they get nervous just before going in to visit Santa. They pace and wring their hands and stare at the floor. They act like they're going in for a job interview. I say, "Don't worry, Santa's not going to judge you. He's very relaxed about that sort of thing. He used to be judgmental but people gave him a hard time about it so he stopped. Trust me, you have nothing to worry about."

          I was Photo Elf tonight for the oldest Santa. Usually their names are written on the water cups they keep hidden away on the toy shelf. Every now and then a Santa will call out for water and an elf will hold the cup while his master drinks through a straw. I looked on the cup and saw no name. We were busy tonight and I had no time for an introduction. This was an outstanding Santa, wild but warm. The moment a family leaves, this Santa, sensing another group huddled upon his doorstep, will begin to sing.

    He sings, "A pretty girl . . . is like a melody."

    The parents and children enter the room, and if there is a girl in the party, Santa will take a look at her, hold his gloved hands to his chest, and fake a massive heart attack — falling back against the cushion and moaning with a combination of pleasure and pain. Then he slowly comes out of it and says, "Elf, Elf . . . are you there?"

    "Yes, Santa, I'm here."

    "Elf, I just had a dream that I was standing before the most beautiful girl in the world. She was right here, in my house."

    Then I say, "It wasn't a dream, Santa. Open your eyes, my friend. She's standing before you."

    Santa rubs his eyes and shakes his head as if he were a parish priest, visited by Christ. "Oh, heavenly day," he says, addressing the child. "You are *the* most beautiful girl I have seen in six hundred and seventeen years."

Then he scoops her into his lap and flatters every aspect of her character. The child is delirious. Santa gestures toward the girl's mother, asking, "Is that your sister I see standing there in the corner?"

"No, that's my mother."

Santa calls the woman over close and asks if she has been a good mother. "Do you tell your daughter that you love her? Do you tell her every day?"

The mothers always blush and say, "I try, Santa."

Santa asks the child to give her mother a kiss. Then he addresses the father, again requesting that he tell the child how much he loves her.

Santa ends the visit, saying, "Remember that the most important thing is to try and love other people as much as they love you."

The parents choke up and often cry. They grab Santa's hand and, on the way out, my hand. They say it was worth the wait. The most severe cases open their wallets and hand Santa a few bucks. We're not supposed to accept tips, but most Santas take the money and wink, tucking it into their boot. This Santa looked at the money as if it were a filthy Kleenex. He closed his eyes and prepared for the next family.

With boys, this Santa plays on their brains: each one is the smartest boy in the world.

The great thing about this Santa is that he never even asks what the children want. Most times he involves the parents to the point where they surrender their urge for documentation. They lay down their video recorders and gather round for the festival of love.

I was the Pointer Elf again this afternoon, one of my favorite jobs. The Pointer stands inside the Magic Tree and appoints available Santa Elves to lead parties of visitors to the houses. First-time visitors are enthusiastic, eager that they are moments away from Santa. Some of the others, having been here before, have decided to leave nothing to chance.

Out of all the Santas, two are black and both are so light-skinned that, with the beard and makeup, you would be hard-pressed to determine their race.

Last week, a black woman became upset when, having requested a "Santa of color," she was sent to Jerome.

After she was led to the house, the woman demanded to speak with a manager.

"He's not black," the woman complained.

Bridget assured this woman that Jerome was indeed black.

The woman said, "Well, he isn't black enough."

Jerome is a difficult Santa, moody and unpredictable. He spends a lot of time staring off into space and tallying up his paycheck for the hours he has worked so far. When a manager ducks in, encouraging him to speed things up, Jerome says,

"Listen up, I'm playing a role here. Do you understand? A dramatic role that takes a great deal of preparation, so don't hassle me about 'Time.'"

Jerome seems to have his own bizarre agenda. When the children arrive, he looks down at his boots and lectures them, suggesting a career in entomology.

"Entomology, do you know what that is?"

He tells them that the defensive spray of the stink bug may contain medicinal powers that can one day cure mankind of communicable diseases.

"Do you know about holistic medicine?" he asks.

The Photo Elf takes a picture of yawning children.

The other black Santa works during weeknights and I have never met him but hear he is a real entertainer, popular with Photo Elves and children.

The last time I was the Pointer Elf, a woman approached me and whispered, "We would like a *traditional* Santa. I'm sure you know what I'm talking about."

I sent her to Jerome.

Yesterday Snowball was the Pointer and a woman pulled him aside, saying, "Last year we had a chocolate Santa. Make sure it doesn't happen again."

I saw it all today. I was Pointer Elf for all of five minutes before a man whispered, "Make sure we get a white one this year. Last year we were stuck with a black."

A woman touched my arm and mouthed, "White — white like *us*."

I address a Santa Elf, the first in line, and hand these people over. Who knows where they will wind up? The children are antsy, excited — they want to see Santa. The children are sweet. The parents are manipulative and should be directed toward the A&S Plaza, two blocks away. A&S has only two Santas working at the same time — a white Santa and a black Santa, and it's very clear-cut: whites in one line and blacks in another.

I've had requests from both sides. White Santa, black Santa, a Pointer Elf is instructed to shrug his shoulders and feign ignorance, saying, "There's only one Santa."

Today I experienced my cash register nightmare. The actual financial transactions weren't so bad — I've gotten the hang of that. The trouble are the voids. A customer will offer to pay in cash and then, after I have arranged it, they examine their wallets and say, "You know what, I think I'll put that on my card instead."

This involves voids and signatures from the management.

I take care of the paperwork, accept their photo form, and staple it to the receipt. Then it is my job to say, "The pictures taken today will be mailed January twelfth."

The best part of the job is watching their faces fall. These pictures are sent to a lab to be processed; it takes time, all these pictures so late in the season. If they wanted their pictures to arrive before Christmas, they should have come during the first week we were open. Lots of people want their money back after learning the pictures will arrive after Christmas, in January, when Christmas is forgotten. Void.

We were very crowded today and I got a kick out of completing the transaction, handing the customer a receipt, and saying, "Your photos will be mailed on August tenth."

August is much funnier than January. I just love to see that look on someone's face, the mouth a perfect O.

This was my last day of work. We had been told that Christmas Eve is a slow day, but this was the day a week of training was meant to prepare us for. It was a day of nonstop action, a day when the managers spent a great deal of time with their walkie-talkies.

I witnessed a fistfight between two mothers and watched while a woman experienced a severe, crowd-related anxiety attack: falling to the floor and groping for breath, her arms moving as though she were fighting off bats. A Long Island father called Santa a faggot because he couldn't take the time to recite "The Night Before Christmas" to his child. Parents in long lines left disposable diapers at the door to Santa's house. It was the rowdiest crowd I have ever seen, and we were short on elves, many of whom simply did not show up or called in sick. As a result we had our lunch hours cut in half and had to go without our afternoon breaks. Many elves complained bitterly, but the rest of us found ourselves in the moment we had all been waiting for. It was us against them. It was time to be a trouper, and I surrendered completely. My Santa and I had them on the lap, off the lap in forty-five seconds flat. We were an efficient machine surrounded by chaos. Quitting time came and went for the both of us and we paid it no mind. My plane was due to leave at eight o'clock, and I stayed until the last moment, figuring the time it would take to get to the airport. It was with reservation that I reported to the manager, telling her I had to leave. She was at a cash register, screaming at a customer. She was, in fact, calling this customer a bitch. I touched her arm and said, "I have to go now." She laid her hand on my shoulder, squeezed it gently, and continued her conversation, saying, "Don't tell the store president I called you a bitch. Tell him I called you a fucking bitch, because that's exactly what you are. Now get out of my sight before I do something we both regret."

Season's Greetings to
Our Friends and Family!!!

Many of you, our friends and family, are probably taken aback by this, our annual holiday newsletter. You've read of our recent tragedy in the newspapers and were no doubt thinking that, what with all of their sudden legal woes and "hassles," the Dunbar clan might just stick their heads in the sand and avoid this upcoming holiday season altogether!!

You're saying, "There's no way the Dunbar family can grieve their terrible loss *and* carry on the traditions of the season. No family is *that* strong," you're thinking to yourselves.

Well, think again!!!!!!!!!!!!

While this past year has certainly dealt our family a heavy hand of sorrow and tribulation, we have (so far!) weathered the storm and shall continue to do so! Our tree is standing tall in the living room, the stockings are hung, and we are eagerly awaiting the arrival of a certain portly gentleman who goes by the name "Saint Nick"!!!!!!!!!!!!

Our trusty PC printed out our wish lists weeks ago and now we're cranking it up again to wish you and yours The Merriest of Christmas Seasons from the entire Dunbar family: Clifford, Jocelyn, Kevin, Jacki, Kyle, and Khe Sahn!!!!!

Some of you are probably reading this and scratching your heads over the name "Khe Sahn." "That certainly doesn't fit with the rest of the family names," you're saying to yourself. "What, did those crazy Dunbars get themselves a Siamese cat?"

You're close.

To those of you who live in a cave and haven't heard the news, allow us to introduce Khe Sahn Dunbar who, at the age of twenty-two, happens to be the newest member of our family.

Surprised?

JOIN THE CLUB!!!!!!!

It appears that Clifford, husband of yours truly and father to our three natural children, accidentally planted the seeds for Khe Sahn twenty-two years ago during his stint in . . . where else?

VIETNAM!!!!

This was, of course, years before Clifford and I were married. At the time of his enlistment we were pre-engaged and the long period of separation took its toll on both of us. I corresponded regularly. (I wrote him every single day, even when I couldn't think of anything interesting. His letters were much less frequent but I saved all four of them!)

While I had both the time and inclination to put my feelings into envelopes, Clifford, along with thousands of other American soldiers, had no such luxury. While the rest of us were watching the evening news in our safe and comfortable homes, he was *making* the evening news, standing waist high in a stagnant foxhole. The hazards and the torments of war are something that, luckily, most of us cannot begin to imagine and, for that, we should all count our blessings.

Clifford Dunbar, twenty-two years ago, a young man in a war-torn country, made a mistake. A terrible, heinous mistake. A stupid, thoughtless, permanent mistake with dreadful, haunting consequences.

But who are you, who are any of us, to judge him for it? Especially now, with Christmas at our heels. Who are we to judge?

When his tour of duty ended Clifford returned home, where, after making the second biggest mistake of his life (I am referring to his brief eight-month "marriage" to Doll Babcock), he and I were reunited. We lived, you might remember, in that tiny apartment over on Halsey Street. Clifford had just begun his satisfying career at Sampson Interlock and I was working part-time, accounting for Hershel Beck when . . . along came the children!!!!!! We struggled and saved and eventually (finally!!) bought our house on

Tiffany Circle, number 714, where the Dunbar clan remains nested to this very day!!!!

It was here, 714 Tiffany Circle, where I first encountered Khe Sahn, who arrived at our door on (as fate would have it) Halloween!!!

I recall mistaking her for a Trick-or-Treater! She wore, I remember, a skirt the size of a beer cozy, a short, furry jacket, and, on her face, enough rouge, eye shadow, and lipstick to paint our entire house, inside and out. She's a very small person and I mistook her for a child. A child masquerading as a prostitute. I handed her a fistful of chocolate nougats, hoping that, like the other children, she would quickly move on to the next house.

But Khe Sahn was no Trick-or-Treater.

I started to close the door but was interrupted by her interpreter, a very feminine-looking man carrying an attaché case. He introduced himself in English and then turned to Khe Sahn, speaking a language I have sadly come to recognize as Vietnamese. While our language flows from our mouths, the Vietnamese language sounds as though it is being forced from the speaker by a series of heavy and merciless blows to the stomach. The words themselves are the sounds of pain. Khe Sahn responded to the interpreter, her voice as high-pitched and relentless as a car alarm. The two of them stood on my doorstep, screeching away in Vietnamese while I stood by, frightened and confused.

I am still, to this day, frightened and confused. Very much so.

DAVID SEDARIS

It is frightening that, after all this time, a full-grown bastard (I use that word technically) can cross the seas and make herself comfortable in my home, all with the blessing of our government. Twenty-two years ago Uncle Sam couldn't stand the Vietnamese. Now he's dressing them like prostitutes and moving them into our houses!!!! Out of nowhere this young woman has entered our lives with the force and mystery of the Swine Flu and there appears to be nothing we can do about it. Out of nowhere this land mine knocks upon our door and we are expected to recognize her as our child!!!!????????

Clifford likes to say that the Dunbar children inherited their mother's looks and their father's brains. It's true: Kevin, Jackelyn, and Kyle are all just as good-looking as they can possibly be! And smart? Well, they're smart enough, smart like their father, with the exception of our oldest son, Kevin. After graduating Moody High with honors, Kevin is currently enrolled in his third year at Feeny State, majoring in chemical engineering. He's made the honor roll every semester and there seems to be no stopping him!!! A year and a half left to go and already the job offers are pouring in!

We love you, Kevin!!!!!!!!!!!!!!!!!!!

We sometimes like to joke that when God handed out brains to the Dunbar kids He saw Kevin standing first in line and awarded him the whole sack!!! What the other children lack in brains they seem to make up for in one way or another. They have qualities and personalities and make observations, unlike Khe Sahn, who seems to believe she can coast through life on her looks alone!! She hasn't got the ambition God gave a sparrow! She arrived in this house six weeks ago speaking only the words "Daddy," "Shiny," and "Five dollar now."

Quite a vocabulary!!!!!!!!!!

While an industrious person might buckle down and seriously study the language of her newly adopted country, Khe Sahn appeared to be in no hurry whatsoever. When asked a simple question such as, "Why don't you go back where you came from?" she would touch my hand and launch into a spasm of Vietnamese drivel — as if I were the outsider, expected to learn *her* language! We were visited several times by Lonnie Tipit, that "interpreter," that "man" who accompanied Khe Sahn on her first visit. Mr. Tipit seemed to feel that the Dunbar door was open for him anytime, day or night. He'd drop by (most often during the supper hours) and, between helpings of *my* home-cooked meals (thank you very much), "touch base" with his "friend," Khe Sahn. "I don't think she's getting enough exposure to the community," he would say. "Why don't you start taking her around town, to church get-togethers and local events?" Well, that was easy for *him* to say! I told him, I said, "*You* try taking a girl in a halter top to a confirmation class. *You* take her to the Autumn Craft Caravan and watch her snatch every shiny object that catches her eye. I've learned my lesson already." Then he and Khe Sahn would confer in Vietnamese and he would listen, his eyes fixed upon me as if I were a witch he had once read about in books but did not recognize without a smoldering kettle and a broom. Oh, I knew that look!

Lonnie Tipit went so far as to suggest that we hire him as Khe Sahn's English tutor at, get this, seventeen dollars an hour!!!!!!!!!! Seventeen dollars an hour so she can learn to lisp and twitter and flutter her hands like two small birds? NO, THANK YOU!!!!!!! Oh, I saw right through Lonnie Tipit. While he pretended to care for Khe Sahn I understood that his true interest was in my son Kyle. "How's the schoolwork coming, Kyle? Working hard or hardly working?" and "Say, Kyle, what do you think about this new sister of yours? Is she the greatest or what?"

It wasn't difficult to see through Lonnie Tipit. He wanted one thing and one thing only. "If not me, then I can suggest another tutor," he said. Someone like who? Someone like him? Regardless of who the English teacher was, I am not in the habit of throwing my money away. And that, my friends, is what it would have amounted to. Why not hire an expensive private tutor to teach the squirrels to speak in French! It would be no more ridiculous than teaching Khe Sahn English. A person has to *want* to learn. I know that. Apparently, back in Ho Chi Minh City, Her Majesty was treated like a queen and sees no reason to change her ways!!!! Her Highness rises at around noon, wolfs down a fish or two (all she eats is fish and chicken breasts), and settles herself before the makeup mirror, waiting for her father to return home from work. At the sound of his car in the driveway she perks up and races to the door like a spaniel, panting and wagging her tail to beat the band! Suddenly she is eager to please and attempt conversation!! Well, I don't know how they behave in Vietnam, but in the United States it is not customary for a half-dressed daughter to offer her father a five-dollar massage!!! After having spent an exhausting day attempting to communicate a list of simple chores, I would stand in amazement at Khe Sahn's sudden grasp of English when faced with my husband.

"Daddy happy five dollar shiny now, OK?"

"You big feet friendly with ABC Khe Sahn. You Big Bird Daddy Grover."

Apparently she had picked up a few words while watching "Sesame Street."

"Daddy special special funky fresh jam party commercial free jam."

She began listening to the radio.

Khe Sahn treats our youngest son, Kyle, with complete indifference, which is probably a blessing in disguise. This entire episode has been very difficult for Kyle, who, at age fifteen, tends to be the artistic loner of the family. He keeps to himself, spending many hours in his bedroom, where he burns incense, listens to music, and carves gnomes out of soap. Kyle is very good-looking and talented and we are looking forward to the day when he sets aside his jackknife and bar of Irish Spring and begins "carving out" a future rather than a shriveled troll! He is at that very difficult age but we pray he will grow out of it and follow his brother's footsteps to success before it is too late. Hopefully, the disasters of his sister, Jackelyn, will open his eyes to the hazards of drugs, the calamity of a thoughtless, premature marriage, and the heartaches of parenthood!

We had, of course, warned our daughter against marrying Timothy Speaks. We warned, threatened, cautioned, advised, what have you — but it did no good as a young girl, with all the evidence before her, sees only what she *wants* to see. The marriage was bad enough but the news of her pregnancy struck her father and me with the force of a hurricane.

Timothy Speaks, the father of our grandchild? How could it be????

Timothy Speaks, who had so many pierced holes in his ears you could have torn the lobe right off, effortlessly ripped it loose the same way you might separate a stamp from a sheet.

Timothy Speaks, who had his back and neck tattooed with brilliant flames. His neck!!!

We told Jacki, "One of these days he's going to have to grow up and find a job, and when he does, those employers are going to wonder why he's wearing a turtleneck under his business suit. People with tattooed necks do not, as a rule, hold down high-paying jobs," we said.

She ran back to Timothy repeating our warning. . . . Lo and behold, two days later, *she* showed up with a tattooed neck as well!!!!! They even made plans to have their baby tattooed!!!! A tattoo, on an infant!!!!!!!!!!!

Timothy Speaks held our daughter in a web of madness that threatened to ensnare the entire Dunbar family. It was as if he held her under a perverse spell, convincing her, little by little, to destroy the lives of those around her.

The Jackelyn Dunbar-Speaks who lived with Timothy in that squalid "space" on West Vericose Avenue bore no resemblance to the beautiful girl pictured in our photo albums. The sensitive and considerate daughter we once knew became, under his fierce coaching, a mean-spirited, unreliable, and pregnant ghost who eventually gave birth to a ticking time bomb!!!!!

We, of course, saw it coming. The child, born September tenth under the influence of drugs, spent the first two months of his life in the critical care unit of St. Joe's Hospital. (At a whopping cost and guess who paid the bill for *that* one?) Faced with the concrete responsibility of fatherhood, Timothy Speaks abandoned his sick wife and child. Suddenly. Gone. Poof!

Surprised?

We saw it coming and are happy to report that, as of this writing, we have no idea where he is or what he is up to. (We could guess, but why bother?)

We have all read the studies and understand that a drug-addicted baby faces a difficult, uphill battle in terms of living a normal life. This child, having been given the legal name "Satan

DAVID SEDARIS

Speaks" would, we felt, have a harder time than most. We were lucky enough to get Jacki into a fine treatment center on the condition that the child remain here with us until which time (if ever) she is able to assume responsibility for him. The child arrived at our home on November tenth and shortly thereafter, following her initial withdrawal, Jacki granted us permission to address it as "Don." Don, a nice, simple name.

The name change enabled us to look upon the baby without having to consider the terrible specter of his father, Timothy Speaks. It made a difference, believe me.

While I could not describe him as being a "normal" baby, taking care of young Don gave me a great deal of pleasure. Terribly insistent, prone to hideous rashes, a twenty-four hour round-the-clock screamer, he was our grandchild and we loved him. Knowing that he would physically grow to adulthood while maintaining the attention span of a common housefly did not, in the least bit, diminish our feelings for him.

Clifford would sometimes joke that Don was a "Crack Baby" because he woke us at the crack of dawn!

I would then take the opportunity to mention that Khe Sahn was something of a "Crack Baby" herself, wandering around our house all hours of the day and night wearing nothing but a pair of hot pants and a glorified sports bra. Most nights, the dinnertime napkin in her lap provided more coverage than she was accustomed to!!! Clifford suggested that I buy her a few decent dresses and a couple pairs of jeans and I tried, oh, how I tried! I sat with her, leafing through catalogs, and watched as she pawed the expensive designer outfits. I walked with her through Cut Throat's and Discount Plus and watched as she turned up her nose at their sensibly priced clothing. I don't know about you, but in *this* family the children are rewarded for hard work. Call me old-fashioned but if you want a fifty-dollar sweater you have to prove that you deserve it! If I've said it once I've said it a thousand times: "A family is not a charitable organization." Khe Sahn wanted something for nothing and I buttoned my purse and said the most difficult word a parent can say, "No!" I made her several outfits, sewed them with my own hands, two floor-length dresses, beautiful burlap dresses, but did she wear them? Of course not!!!

She continued in her usual fashion, trotting about the house in her underwear! When the winter winds began to blow she took to draping herself in a bed blanket, huddling beside the fireplace. While her "Poor Little Match Girl" routine might win a Tony Award on Broadway it did nothing for this ticket holder!

She carried on, following at Clifford's heels, until Thanksgiving Day, when she was introduced to our son Kevin, home for the holiday. One look at Kevin and it was "Clifford? Clifford who?" as far as Khe Sahn was concerned. One look at our handsome son and the "Shivering Victim" dropped her blanket and showed her true colors. It is a fact that she appeared at our Thanksgiving table wearing nothing but a string bikini!!!!!!!!!

"Not in *my* house," said yours truly! When I demanded she change into one of the dresses I had sewn for her, Khe Sahn frowned into her cranberry sauce, pretending not to understand. Clifford and Kevin tried to convince me that, in Vietnam, it is customary for the women to wear swimsuits on Thanksgiving Day but I still don't believe a word of it. Since when do the Vietnamese observe Thanksgiving? What do those people have to be thankful for?

She ruined our holiday dinner with her giggling, coy games. She sat beside Kevin until, insisting she had seen a spider in her chair, she moved into his lap!! "You new funky master jam party mix silly fresh spider five dollar Big Bird."

Those of you who know Kevin understand that, while he is an absolute whip at some things, he is terribly naive at others. Tall and good-looking, easy with a smile and a kind word, Kevin has been the target of many a huntress. He is both smart and foolish: it is his gift and his weakness, bound together, constantly struggling for control. He has always had more than his fair share of opportunists, both at Moody High and Feeny State. Always the gentleman, he treated the young ladies like glass, which, looking back, was appropriate because you could see through each and every one of them. When he asked to bring a date home for Thanksgiving I said I thought it was a bad idea as we were all under more than enough stress already. Looking back, I wish he *had* brought a date, as it might have dampened the sky-high hopes and aspirations of Khe Sahn, his half-sister!!!!!!!!!!

"Me no big big potato spoon fork tomorrow? Kevin have big big shiny face like hand of chicken soon with funky crazy Sesame Street jammy jam."

I could barely choke down my meal and found myself counting the minutes before Kevin, the greatest joy of our lives, called an end to the private English lesson he gave Khe Sahn in her bedroom, got into his car, and returned to Feeny State.

As I mentioned before, Kevin has always been a very caring person, always going out of his way to lend a hand or comfort a stranger. Being as that is his nature, he returned to school and, evidently, began phoning Khe Sahn, sometimes speaking with the aid of a Vietnamese student who acted as an interpreter. He was, in his own way, foolishly trying to make her feel welcome and adjust to life in her new, highly advanced country. He even went out of his way to drive all the way home in order to take her out and introduce her to the ways of nightlife in this, her adopted land. That is the Kevin we all know and love, always trying to help a person less intelligent than himself, bending over backwards to coax a smile!

Unfortunately, Khe Sahn misinterpreted his interest as a declaration of romantic concern. She took to "manning" the telephone twenty-four hours a day, hovering above it and regarding it as though it were a living creature. Whenever (God forbid!) someone called for Clifford, Kyle, or me, she would simply hang up!!!!

How's *that* for an answering service!!!!!!!!!!!!!!

Eventually, recognizing that her behavior bordered on insanity, I had a word with her.

"HE'S NOT FOR YOU," I yelled. (I have been criticized for yelling, told that it doesn't serve any real purpose when speaking to a foreigner, but at least it gets their attention!) "HE'S MY SON IN COLLEGE. MY SON ON THE DEAN'S LIST, NOT FOR YOU."

She was perched beside the telephone with a curling iron in her hand. At the sound of my voice she instinctively turned her attention elsewhere.

"BOTH MY SON AND MY HUSBAND ARE OFF-LIMITS AS FAR AS YOU'RE CONCERNED, DO YOU UNDERSTAND? THEY ARE EACH RELATED TO YOU IN ONE WAY OR ANOTHER AND THAT MAKES IT WRONG. AUTOMATICALLY WRONG. BAD, BAD, WRONG! WRONG AND BAD TOGETHER FOR THE KHE SAHN TO BE WITH JOCELYN'S SON OR HUSBAND. BAD AND WRONG. DO YOU UNDERSTAND WHAT I AM SAYING NOW?"

She looked up for a moment or two before returning her attention to the electrical cord.

I gave up. Trying to explain moral principles to Khe Sahn was like reviewing a standard 1040 tax form with a house cat! She understands only what she chooses to understand. Say the word "shopping" and, quicker than you can blink, she's sitting in the front seat of the car! Try a more complicated word such as "sweep" or "iron" and she shrugs her shoulders and retreats to the bedroom.

"VACUUM," I would say. "VACUUM THE CARPET."

In response she would jangle her bracelet or observe her fingernails.

In a desperate attempt to make myself understood I would pull out the vacuum cleaner and demonstrate.

"LOOK AT JOCELYN. JOCELYN VACUUMS THE CARPET. LA LA LA!! IT IS MUCH FUN TO VACUUM. IT IS AN ENJOYMENT AND A PLEASURE TO CLEAN MY HOME WITH A VACUUM. LA LA LA!!"

I tried to convey it as a rewarding exercise but, by the time I finally sparked her interest I was finished with the job.

As I said earlier, Khe Sahn understands only what she wants to understand. Looking back, I suppose I had no valid reason to trust her sudden willingness to lend a hand but, on the day in question, I was nearing the end of my rope.

We were approaching Christmas, December sixteenth, when I made the thoughtless mistake of asking her to watch the child while I ran some errands. With a needy, shriveled newborn baby, a teenaged son, and a twenty-two-year-old, half-dressed "stepdaughter" in my house, my hands were full from one moment to the next, twenty-eight hours a day!!!! It was nine days before Christmas and, busy as I was, I hadn't bought a single gift. (Santa, where are you????????)

On that early afternoon Kyle was in school, Clifford was at the office, and Khe Sahn was seated beside the telephone, picking at a leftover baked fish with her bare hands.

"WATCH THE BABY," I said. "WATCH DON, THE BABY, WHILE I GO OUT."

She considered her greasy fingers.

"YOU WATCH BABY DON WHILE JOCELYN GOES SHOPPING FOR SPECIAL PRESENT FOR THE KHE SAHN!" I said. "HO, HO, HO, SPECIAL CHRISTMAS FOR THE KHE SAHN, HO, HO!"

At the mention of the word "shopping" she perked up and gave me her full attention. Having heard the radio and watched TV, she understood Christmas as an opportunity to receive gifts and was in the habit of poring over the mail-order catalogs and expressing her desires with the words, "Ho, ho, ho."

I clearly remember my choice of words on that cold and cloudy December afternoon. I did not say "baby-sit," fearing that she might take me at my word and literally sit upon the baby.

"WATCH THE BABY," I said to that twenty-two-year-old adult on the afternoon of December sixteenth.

"WATCH THE BABY," I said as we climbed the stairs toward the bedroom that she and Don shared. Khe Sahn had been sleeping in Kevin's vacant bedroom until, following her Thanksgiving high jinks, I decided to move her into the nursery with Don.

"WATCH THE BABY," I repeated as we stood over the crib and observed the wailing infant. I picked him up and rocked him gently as he struggled in my arms. "WATCH BABY."

"Watch Baby," Khe Sahn responded, holding out her arms to

accept him. "Watch Baby for Jocelyn get shop special HO, HO, HO, Khe Sahn fresh shiny."

"Exactly," I said, laying a hand on her shoulder.

How foolish I was to have honestly believed that she was finally catching on! I was, at that moment in time, convinced of her sincerity. I was big enough to set aside all of the trouble she had visited upon our household and give her another chance! *That is all behind us now*, I said to myself, watching her cradle the wailing child.

Oh, what a fool I was!!!!!!!!!!!!!

Leaving the house and driving toward White Paw Center I felt a sense of relief I had not known in quite a while. This was the first time in weeks I had allowed myself a moment alone and, with six Dunbar wish lists burning a hole in my pocket, I intended to make the most of it!!!

I can't account for every moment of my afternoon. Never did it occur to me that I would one day be called upon to do so but, that being the case, I will report what I remember. I can comfortably testify that, on the afternoon of December sixteenth, I visited the White Paw Shopping Center, where I spent a brief amount of time in The Slack Heap, searching for a gift for Kyle. I found what he wanted but not in his size. I then left The Slack Heap and walked over to ———————— & ——— ————————, where I bought a ———————— for my daughter Jacki. (I'm not going to ruin anyone's Christmas surprises here. Why should I?) I stuck my head inside Turtleneck Crossing and searched for candles at Wax and Wane. I bought a gift for Clifford at ——————, and I suppose I browsed. There are close to a hundred shops at the White Paw Center and you'll have to forgive me if I can't provide a detailed list of how long I spent in this or that store. I shopped until I grew wary of the time. On the way home I stopped at The Food Carnival and bought a few items. It was getting dark, perhaps four-thirty, when I pulled into the driveway of our home on Tiffany Circle. I collected my packages from the car and entered my home, where I was immediately struck by the eerie silence. "This doesn't feel right to me," I remember saying to myself. It was an intuition, a mother's intuition, that unexplainable language of the senses. I laid down my bags and was startled by the sound they made — the crisp noise of paper bags settling against the floor. The problem was that I could hear the sound at all! Normally I would have heard nothing over the chronic bleating of Baby Don and the incessant blaring radio of Khe Sahn.

Something is wrong, I said to myself. *Something is terribly, terribly wrong.*

Before calling out for Khe Sahn or checking on the baby I instinctively phoned the police. I then stood there, stock-still in the living room, staring at my shopping bags until they arrived (twenty-seven minutes later!!).

At the sound of the squad car in the driveway, Khe Sahn made an entrance, parading down the stairs in a black lace half-slip and a choker made from the cuff of Kevin's old choir robe.

"WHERE IS THE BABY?" I asked her. "WHERE IS DON?"

Accompanied by the police we went upstairs into the nursery and stood beside the empty crib.

"WHERE IS MY GRANDCHILD, DON? WHAT HAVE YOU DONE TO THE BABY?"

Khe Sahn, of course, said nothing. It is part of her act to tug at her hemline and feign shyness when first confronted by strangers. We left her standing there while the police and I began our search. We combed the entire house, the officers and I, before finally finding the helpless baby in the laundry room, warm but lifeless in the dryer.

The autopsy later revealed that Don had also been subjected to a wash cycle — hot wash, cold rinse. He died long before the spin cycle, which is, I suppose, the only blessing to be had in this entire ugly episode. I am still, to this day, haunted by the mental picture of my grandchild undergoing such brutality. The relentless pounding he received during his forty-five minutes in the dryer is something I would rather not think about. The thought of it visits me like a nightmare! It comes repeatedly to my mind and I put my hands to my head, desperately trying to drive it away. One wishes for an only grandchild to run and play, to graduate from college, to marry and succeed, not to . . . (see, I can't even say it!!!!!!).

The shock and horror that followed Don's death are something I would rather not recount: Calling our children to report the news, watching the baby's body, small as a loaf of bread, as it was zipped into a heavy plastic bag — these images have nothing to do with the merriment of Christmas, and I hope my mention of them will not dampen your spirits at this, the most special and glittering time of the year.

The evening of December sixteenth was a very dark hour for the Dunbar family. At least with Khe Sahn in police custody we could grieve privately, consoling ourselves with the belief that justice had been carried out.

How foolish we were!!!!!!!!!!!!

The bitter tears were still wet upon our faces when the police returned to Tiffany Circle, where they began their ruthless questioning of Yours Truly!!!!!!!!!!!! Through the aid of an interpreter, Khe Sahn had spent a sleepless night at police headquarters, constructing a story of unspeakable lies and betrayal! While I am not at liberty to discuss her exact testimony, allow me to voice my disappointment that anyone (let alone the police!) would even *think* of taking Khe Sahn's word over my own. How could I have placed a helpless child in the washing machine? Even if I were cruel enough to do such a thing, when would I have found the time? I was out shopping.

You may have read that our so-called "neighbor" Cherise Clarmont-Shea reported that she witnessed me leaving my home at around one-fifteen on the afternoon of December sixteenth and then, twenty minutes later, allegedly park my car on the far corner of Tiffany and Papageorge and, in her words, "creep" through her backyard and in through my basement door!!!!!! Cherise Clarmont-Shea certainly understands the meaning of the word *creep*, doesn't she? She's been married to one for so long that she has turned into something of a creep herself!! How many times have I opened the door to Cherise, her face swollen and mustard-colored, suffering another of her husband's violent slugfests! She's been smacked in the face so many times she's lucky if she can see anything through those swollen eyes of hers! If the makeup she applies is any indication of her vision, then I believe it is safe to say she can't see two inches in front of her, much less testify to the identity of someone she might think she's seen crossing her yard. She's on pills, everyone knows that. She's desperate for attention and I might pity her under different circumstances. I did not return home early and creep through the Sheas' unkept backyard, but even if I had, what possible motive would I have had? Why would I, as certain people have been suggesting, want to murder my own grandchild? This is madness, pure and simple. It reminds me of a recurring nightmare I often have wherein I am desperately trying to defend myself against a heavily armed hand puppet. The grotesque puppet angrily accuses me of spray-painting slogans on his car. I have, of course, done no such thing. *This is insane, preposterous*, I think to myself. "This makes no sense," I say, all the while eyeing the loaded weapon in his small hands and praying for this nightmare to end. Cherise Clarmont-Shea has no more sense than a hand puppet. She has three names! And the others who have made statements against me, Chaz Staples and Vivian Taps, they were both at home during a weekday afternoon doing guess what while their spouses were hard at work. What are *they* hiding? I feel it is of utmost importance to consider the source.

These charges are ridiculous, yet I must take them seriously as my very life may be at stake! Listening to a taped translation of Khe Sahn's police statement, the Dunbar family has come to fully understand the meaning of the words "controlling," "vindictive," "manipulative," "greedy," and, in a spiritual sense, "ugly."

Not exactly the words one wishes to toss about during the Christmas season!!!!!!!!

A hearing has been set for December twenty-seventh and, knowing how disappointed you, our friends, might feel at being left out, I have included the time and address at the bottom of this letter. The hearing is an opportunity during which you might convey your belated Christmas spirit through deed and action. Given the opportunity to defend *your* character I would not hesitate and I know you must feel the exact same way toward me. That heartfelt concern, that desire to stand by your friends and family, is the very foundation upon which we celebrate the Christmas season, isn't it?

While this year's Dunbar Christmas will be seasoned with loss and sadness, we plan to proceed, as best we can, toward that day of days, December twenty-seventh — 1:45 P.M. at The White Paw County Courthouse, room 412.

I will be calling to remind you of that information and look forward to discussing the festive bounty of your holiday season.

Until that time we wish the best to you and yours.

Merry Christmas,

The Dunbars

Front Row Center with Thaddeus Bristol

Trite Christmas: Scottsfield's young hams offer the blandest of holiday fare

The approach of Christmas signifies three things: bad movies, unforgivable television, and even worse theater. I'm talking bone-crushing theater, the type our ancient ancestors used to oppress their enemies before the invention of the stretching rack. We're talking torture on a par with the Scottsfield Dinner Theater's 1994 revival of *Come Blow Your Horn*, a production that violated every tenet of the Human Rights Accord. To those of you who enjoy the comfort of a nice set of thumbscrews, allow me to recommend any of the crucifying holiday plays and pageants currently eliciting screams of mercy from within the confines of our local elementary and middle schools. I will, no doubt, be taken to task for criticizing the work of children but, as any pathologist will agree, if there's a cancer it's best to treat it as early as possible.

If you happened to stand over four feet tall, the agony awaiting you at Sacred Heart Elementary began the moment you took your seat. These were mean little chairs corralled into a "theater" haunted by the lingering stench of industrial-strength lasagna. My question is not why they chose to stage the production in a poorly disguised cafeteria, but why they chose to stage it at all. "The Story of the First Christmas" is an overrated clunker of a holiday pageant, best left to those looking to cure their chronic insomnia. Although the program listed no director, the apathetic staging suggested the limp, partially paralyzed hand of Sister Mary Elizabeth Bronson, who should have been excommunicated after last season's disastrous Thanksgiving program. Here again the first-through third-grade actors graced the stage with an enthusiasm most children reserve for a smallpox vaccination. One could hardly blame them for their lack of vitality, as the stingy, uninspired script consists, not of springy dialogue, but rather of a deadening series of pronouncements.

Mary to Joseph: "I am tired."
Joseph to Mary: "We will rest here for the night."

There's no fire, no give and take, and the audience soon grows weary of this passionless relationship.

In the role of Mary, six-year-old Shannon Burke just barely manages to pass herself off as a virgin. A cloying, preening stage presence, her performance seemed based on nothing but an annoying proclivity toward lifting her skirt and, on rare occasions, opening her eyes. As Joseph, second-grade student Douglas Trazzare needed to be reminded that, although his character did not technically impregnate the virgin mother, he should behave as though he were capable of doing so. Thrown into the mix were a handful of inattentive shepherds and a trio of gift-bearing seven-year-olds who could probably give the Three Stooges a run for their money. As for the lighting, Sacred Heart Elementary chose to rely on nothing more than the flashbulbs ignited by the obnoxious stage mothers and fathers who had created those zombies staggering back and forth across the linoleum-floored dining hall. Under certain circumstances parental pride is understandable but it has no place in the theater, where it tends to encourage a child to believe in a talent that, more often than not, simply fails to exist. In order for a pageant to work, it needs to appeal to everyone, regardless of their relationship to the actors onstage. This production found me on the side of the yawning cafeteria workers.

Pointing to the oversized crate that served as a manger, one particularly insufficient wise man proclaimed, "A child is bored."

Yes, well, so was this adult.

Ten-year-old Charles St. Claire showed great promise with last year's "Silent Falls the Snow." Now he's returned to the holiday well and, finding it empty, presents us with the rusty bucket titled "A Reindeer's Gift," currently running at Scottsfield

Elementary. The story's sentimentality is matched only by its predictability, and the dialogue fills the auditorium like an unrefrigerated boxcar of month-old steaks. The plot, if I may use that word so loosely, involves a boy named Jeremy (Billy Squires) who waits beside the family hearth for . . . guess who! When Santa eventually arrives, he chows down a few cookies and presents our hero with a stack of high-tech treasures. But Jeremy doesn't want gadgetry, he wants a reindeer. Strong-armed into submission, Santa agrees to leave behind his old warhorse Blitzen (played by a lumbering, disobedient Great Dane the program lists as "Marmaduke II"). Left alone with his rowdy charge, Jeremy struggles with his pea-sized conscience, finally realizing that "Maybe it's wrong to keep a reindeer cooped up in the storage space above my stepfather's den." What follows is a tearful good-bye lasting roughly the same length of time it takes a giant redwood to grow from seed to full maturity. By the time the boy returns the reindeer to Santa's custody, we no longer care whether the animal lives or dies. I was just happy he was hustled offstage before his digestive system could process and void the eighteen pounds of popcorn it took to keep the great beast from wandering off before his cue. At the risk of spoiling things for any of our retarded theatergoers, allow me to reveal that the entire Santa–reindeer encounter was nothing more than a dream. Our hero awakes full of Christmas spunk, a lesson is learned, blah, blah, blah.

The only bright spot in the entire evening was the presence of

Kevin "Tubby" Matchwell, the eleven-year-old porker who tackled the role of Santa with a beguiling authenticity. The false beard tended to muffle his speech, but they could hear his chafing thighs all the way to the North Pole. Still, though, the overwrought production tended to mirror the typical holiday meal in that even the Butterball can't save the day when it's packed with too much stuffing.

Once again, the sadists at the Jane Snow-Hernandez Middle School have taken up their burning pokers in an attempt to prod A *Christmas Carol* into some form of submission. I might have overlooked the shoddy production values and dry, leaden pacing, but these are sixth-graders we're talking about and they should have known better. There's really no point in adapting this Dickensian stinker unless you're capable of looking beyond the novel's dime-store morality and getting to what little theatrical meat the story has to offer. The point is to eviscerate the gooey center but here it's served up as the entrée, and a foul pudding it is. Most of the blame goes to the director, eleven-year-old Becky Michaels, who seems to have picked up her staging secrets from the school's crossing guard. She tends to clump her actors, moving them only in groups of five or more. A strong proponent of trendy, racially mixed casting, Michaels gives us a black Tiny Tim, leaving the audience to wonder, "What, is this kid supposed to be adopted?" It's a distracting move, wrongheaded and pointless. The role was played by young Lamar Williams, who, if nothing else, managed to sustain a decent limp. The program notes that he recently lost his right foot to diabetes, but was that reason enough to cast him? As Tiny Tim, the boy spends his stage time essentially trawling for sympathy, stealing focus from even the brightly lit Exit sign. Bob Cratchit, played here by the aptly named Benjamin Trite, seems to have picked up his Cockney accent from watching a few videotaped episodes of "Hee-Haw," and Hershel Fleishman's Scrooge was almost as lame as Tiny Tim.

The set was not without its charm but Jodi Lennon's abysmal costumes should hopefully mark the end of a short and unremarkable career. I was gagging from the smell of spray-painted sneakers and if I see one more top hat made from an oatmeal canister, I swear I'm going to pull out a gun.

The problem with all of these shows stems partially from their maddening eagerness to please. With smiles stretched tight as bungee cords, these hopeless amateurs pranced and gamboled across our local stages, hiding behind their youth and begging, practically demanding, we forgive their egregious mistakes. The English language was chewed into a paste, missed opportunities came and went, and the sets were changed so slowly you'd think the stagehands were encumbered by full-body casts. While billing themselves as holiday entertainment, none of these productions came close to capturing the spirit of Christmas. This glaring irony seemed to escape the throngs of ticketholders, who ate these undercooked turkeys right down to the bone. Here were audiences that chuckled at every technical snafu and applauded riotously each time a new character wandered out onto the stage. With the close of every curtain they leapt to their feet in one ovation after another, leaving me wedged into my doll-sized chair and wondering, "Is it just them, or am I missing something?"

Based Upon a True Story

Good morning, People, and Merry Christmas. Seeing as your minister, Brother Phil Becky, is running a bit late, I thought I'd take this opportunity to say a few words before he wheels himself in to begin the traditional holiday service.

So here I am, Folks, filling in for Phil! (Pause for laughs.) "Who *is* this guy with his hand-tailored Savile Row suit?" you're asking yourselves. Those of you with little or no education are no doubt scratching your heads thinking, "We ain't never seed him before. How you reckon he keeps his shoes so clean?"

Now, Friends, don't get me wrong. I'm not criticizing the way you talk. In fact, I kind of like it. As a people you so-called hillbillies have made a remarkable contribution to the entertainment industry and I, for one, thank you for that.

So who am I? For those of you who don't know me, my name is Jim Timothy and, as you've probably gathered by my full set of

God-given teeth, I'm not from around these parts. Now, Brothers and Sisters, I'm not going to stand up on this pulpit and lie to you. The fact is that I've never preached a sermon in my life, haven't even set foot inside a church since I married my third wife, a blue-eyed Gila monster named Stephanie Concord. Seeing as most of you either can't or don't read the papers, allow me to inform you that Stephanie Concord and I are no longer an item, a fact for which I regularly get down on my hands and knees and, as you people would say, "praise the Lord." What troubles me, what strikes me as grossly unfair, is that the divorce granted that man-eating reptile one half of the money I'd earned during our brief and unrewarding union. I don't want to appear ostentatious, but her settlement amounted to a pretty big chunk of change, seeing as I draw an annual salary that would make your heads spin. You see, Folks, I work in the television industry. No, I'm not a repairman (ha ha) but what you call an executive producer. I guess you could call me the guy who makes it all happen.

Due to my highly advanced sense of humor, I spent the first ten years of my career developing situation comedies, or what we in the business like to refer to as "sit-coms." It was me who helped create such programs as "Eight on a Raft," "Darn Those Fleishmans," "The Dating Cave," and "Crackers 'n' Company," a show you are probably familiar with about a group of ignorant rednecks such as yourself, and I mean that in a good way. According to Old Man Webster, ignorant means "lacking in knowledge and experience," which, let me tell you, can be something of a blessing. There's not a day that passes when I don't spend a few moments wondering if some of us aren't just a little too smart for our own good. You people, with your simple, unremarkable lives, know nothing about production schedules or the sky-high salaries demanded by certain so-called entertainers who could give the Arabs themselves a few pointers on terrorism. I, on the other hand, know nothing about scabies, so maybe we're even.

You don't climb to the top of the sit-com ladder without knowing how to understand people and what makes them tick. I'm not talking about the production assistant tying up the phone lines to weep about her latest abortion. I'm talking about *real* people with weatherbeaten faces and just a little bit of dirt beneath their nails. You have to be able to relate to the little guy because *that's* what makes a television program take off and fly. You can have all the gags in the world, but without that little kernel of understanding you might as well take your project and throw it up on the stage where nobody will ever see it.

A wise man once said that in order to communicate, you have to be able to speak in someone else's language. Take me, for instance. Here I've been rattling off terms such as "Folks" and "Brothers and Sisters" when I would never, and I mean *never*, use such language in a more sophisticated setting. But I use it here, in this run-down church, because, in order to communicate, I need to speak your language. I did the same during a recent visit to London, where, within the course of a single weekend, I found myself using the words "bloody" and "tuppence." In short, I'm a communicator.

Due in large part to my extraordinary interpersonal relationship skills, I was eventually snatched up by a rival network and put in charge of dramatic programming. No, I'm not talking about the vapid soap operas people like you tend to enjoy. I'm referring to the hard-hitting, socially relevant, and meaningful programs that reflect what's really going on in this country of ours. Without a laugh track or a standard twenty-two-minute time frame, these are the shows that touch your heart rather than tickle your funny bone. Maybe they cause you to shed a tear or two, but at least you'll walk away feeling a sense of pride in our shared heritage. These are the programs in which good-looking people attempt to cope with a life which, as many of you obviously know, isn't always as pretty as you'd like it to be. Sometimes these good-looking people are forced to visit poorly decorated homes or even trailers. Every now and then they come into contact with people who aren't so good-looking, but still they're forced to cope. Just as we all do. I'm talking about such award-winning programs as "Coping with the Cavanaughs," "Cynthia Chinn: Oriental Wet Nurse," "Hal's Tumor," and "White Like Me." (Hold for applause.)

Stand in any one place for too long and a person is bound to get itchy feet. I found my voice with situation comedies, proved myself with dramas, and felt it was time to move on to the ratings boosters we like to call the "mini-series." I'm sure at least a few of you are familiar with the concept. They're called "mini" when, in fact, they tend to be much longer than a standard movie you'd see at the local theater. Part of this is due to the commercials, but it's also our chance to dig in our heels and get to the real meat of the story. Sometimes these programs are based upon the novels written by many of your favorite authors, such as James Chutney and Jocelyn Hershey-Guest. I like to think we did real justice to Olivia Hightop's "Midnight's Cousin," and E. Thomas Wallop's searing historical saga "The Business End of the Stick." As I said, often these mini-series are based upon works of fiction, but just as frequently we can find equally compelling material simply by opening our daily newspapers, contacting the survivors or perpetrators, and buying their stories, which are then adapted by any number of our skilled writers. This was the case with "The Boiling of Sister Katherine," a tragic event which I think we explored with a great deal of dignity. Seeing as the nun in question was no longer with us, we bought the rights from the McCracken twins, who, regardless of their guilt or innocence, were an invaluable help to our writers, whose motto is "It's always important to present at least one side of the story." We recently aired another heartbreaking true-life drama, this one based upon a single mother forced to drown her own children, driving them into a lake in a desperate attempt to hold on to her handsome new boyfriend. "Sun Roof Optional" touched a lot of nerves and I was proud to be a part of it.

While the mini-series based upon novels generate a good deal of interest, it's these real-life dramas that tend to draw a larger audience. Why? I chalk it up to five simple words we use in every print or televised promotion. Five words: "Based Upon a True Story." Not made up in the mind of some typist, but *true*. Some say that truth is stranger than fiction, and I usually take that to mean they've spent a few hours with one of my former wives! (Hold for laughs.) Seriously though, nothing touches the heart and mind better than a well-timed dramatization of a real-life event. There also happens to be a fair amount of money in it for the savvy criminal or unfortunate victim who wants to turn his or her grief into something with a lot more buying power than a tearstained pillow! For this reason, we receive hundreds, sometimes thousands, of letters a day from people wanting to sell their true-life experiences. Our network alone has got a basement full of talented college graduates whose job it is to sit on their duffs and evaluate these typed and handwritten tales of woe. We get so many submissions, they're no longer bothering to open any envelope unless the return address includes the name of one of our more notorious state or federal prisons. That's not to say that the other stories aren't compelling in their own way, but we feel these vague accounts of self-doubt and garden-variety adultery are best left to public TV, which has built its reputation on satisfying the needs of a less demanding audience.

"Yes, Mr. Timothy, that's all very interesting, but what does it have to do with Christmas and where the H. E. Double Tooth-picks is Brother Phil Becky?" I'm getting to that.

As I've explained, we've got our dramas and our mini-series and then, ever mindful of the calendar, we've also got our holiday specials. You've no doubt seen or heard of them: "Vince Flatwood's Christmas in Cambodia," or "Kristmus Rappin' with Extraneous B.V.D. and the Skeleton Crew." I could go on and on. Then there are the time-honored animated classics we'll continue to broadcast as long as the toy manufacturers feel a need to advertise the latest video game or lifelike doll that defecates edible figs. I'm not putting these programs down because they all fill their niche. But every now and then — and it's rare — once every blue moon we come upon a marriage of the true-life mini-series *and* the holiday special and that is what we in the television industry like to call "Art."

Our viewers saw Art last Easter with the two-part "Somebody's on My Cross" and they saw it again in "A Wishbone for Li'l Sleepy," in which a hardened gang member carjacks two Dutch tourists so that he can spend Thanksgiving on his grandfather's turkey farm. Both these programs won Emmy Awards on the basis of their hard-hitting portrayal of typical American life. They showed a different side of the coin from your standard "I call the drumstick" or "Santa needs a hand and I'm just the guy to help out" type of thing. This creature we call Art is just as special as the day we call Christmas and you people wouldn't be sitting here if you didn't agree with me. Because Christmas isn't some meaningless postal holiday devoted to the memory of this African American or that guy who got a few boats together and accidentally discovered America. Christmas is about *sharing*. We take what we have and we portion it out to the people who matter in our lives, be they a family member or just some second-string joke writer we drew as a secret Santa. The point is that we *give* and we *take*. It's the oldest story in the book. And that's what brings me here to you very special people on this frigid Christmas morning. I could be with my two stepchildren in San Tocino Del Rey. Or with my natural child at her treatment center at an undisclosed location, or visiting any of the "Two Cents for Hope" kids I foster down in Central America. I could be with my elderly mother in her nursing home or my only brother in wherever he happens to be. But instead I'm here in Jasper's Breath, Kentucky, because, Goddamn it, this is where I want to be! (Pound table, reading stand, whatever they happen to have. Pound forehead if no other options.)

I'm standing before you, the congregation of this simple, shack-like, Pentacostal church, because I care. I care about all of us. Now, I'm not stupid and I won't pretend to be. I read the papers and magazines and know full well that one of your members is somewhat famous. She gave unto her only son a very special Christmas gift. I'm sure you know what I'm talking about. (Smile at woman in question.) A court order prevents me from saying her name but you know who she is. She's seated right now in this very room. Oh, she drew quite a bit of attention one year ago today when she presented her child with the greatest gift a person can give: the gift of life. Being local people you are all no doubt familiar with the story but please allow me to recount it in my own way because I like the *sound* of it. Call me crazy, but this story *does* something to me. One year ago on a frosty Christmas morning, a young widowed mother, poor as dirt but still attractive in her own way, took drastic measures in order to save the life of a five-year-old child who was dying of kidney failure. She had no health insurance or dialysis machine but she did have a heavy Bible which she used to whack the boy against the back of the head, knocking him out in order to spare him the pain that would follow. Taking a rusty penknife and a simple, dime-store sewing kit, the young woman proceeded to remove one of her kidneys and successfully transplant the vital organ into her son's vulnerable body. She did this with no prior experience, completely ignorant of even the simplest of medical procedures. The child had a different blood type and the kidney was much too large for his body but still the organ took, defying all laws of science. This operation was performed not in a sterile surgical environment, but in a dark and dingy hay-filled barn not unlike a manger. There was manure in that barn. There were spiders and fleas but still the transplant was a success. The boy awoke and shortly afterwards was noticed happily playing in the bramble-filled ditch which constituted his front yard. A neighbor contacted the authorities, who were understandably stunned and baffled by the child's complete recovery. When asked how she had managed to perform such complex and delicate surgery, the ignorant young woman said only, "I done it with the help of the Lord."

Now either she's the biggest liar since my third wife, or a miracle took place in that squalid, tin-roofed barn, a miracle witnessed only by two goats, half a dozen chickens, and a gamecock with a broken leg. And unfortunately these animals, like the young woman herself, are refusing to talk. Reporters crawled out of the woodwork, nosing around for answers, but still she held her tongue. A world conference of surgeons flew in from the four corners of the earth and again, all she said was "I done it with the help of the Lord." How's that for some technical mumbo jumbo!

Now, Folks, I can understand this frightened, law-abiding, modest countrywoman turning away the wolves from the tabloids who only want to feature her as the current freak of the week alongside the camel who thinks he's a kitten or the fat man lifted by a crane through the roof of his trailer. These tabloids only want to exploit. They don't understand this woman and her life. They don't understand *you*, let alone someone like me. If you want my opinion, they're nothing but savages and we'd be better off without them. Forgive me if I've offended anyone but sometimes a person just has to let loose and speak his mind.

Let me point out that there are quite a few perplexing questions involving this incident. For example, isn't it funny how this poverty-stricken young widow could have an attorney but not a washing machine? That's right, she's being counseled by her brother, who just barely managed to pass the state bar exam after attending some fourth-rate state college. The man is a loser but he calls himself a lawyer. Go figure. She's been charged with no crime but still I can understand her desire to be counseled and protected. Her brother is a public defender, a man who chooses to spend his life representing thieves and rapists. Here's a guy who sits down and shares his sandwich with the scum of the earth, and *he's* advising this young woman on how to lead her life?

Now I'm not putting down lawyers, I've got a whole team of them myself. They help me out every time I need a divorce or sign the lease on a new ranch or pied-à-terre. They defend me when I'm wrongly accused and they also advise me in terms of money because that's what a good lawyer can do, protect you from making bad choices.

Let me break this down into terms you might be able to understand. Let's say that someone offers to buy your prize piglet for seven dollars. Now maybe that would cause your ears to prick up, but a good lawyer would advise you to wait and see what other offers might come in. Two days later Scat Turdly may want to give you twelve dollars for that piglet, and the day after that Old Man Warner might promise to pay you twenty dollars. The point is that you want to take the best offer but at the same time you've got to think fast. Wait too long and that prize piglet will grow into a bearded old sow with none of its youthful charm. It's like that with stories as well. Sit on something too long and eventually you won't be able to give it away, much less sell it. Now a good lawyer is graced with a keen sense of timing forged by years of experience in the entertainment industry. A good lawyer seizes the moment and closes a deal that will benefit both himself and his client. A bad, self-serving public defender will do no such thing. This young woman's brother has foolishly respected his client's desire to turn down *all* offers in regard to her story. Even worse, he's placed a restraining order against the very people who are trying to help bring this story out from the shadows and into the light. I can understand turning away the book and motion-picture people, but this is TV we're talking about! (Slap Bible for emphasis.) Someone less scrupulous than myself could produce an unauthorized version of this story, maybe shifting a detail or two in order to avoid a crippling lawsuit. They could, for instance, make a two-hour television movie about a Buddhist grandmother who transplants a spleen while kneeling in a pup tent over the long Fourth of July weekend, but me, personally, I don't want to do that.

The fact of the matter is, that until this young woman agrees to sit down and reason with us, we *have* no story because, without her cooperation, there's no way of knowing what really took place in that godforsaken barn on the morning of Christmas one year ago today. And it's a tragedy that her son is no longer available to fill in the missing pieces. Here this woman sacrificed one of her own kidneys in order to save the boy's life and six days later he was struck down by a remote location satellite truck. Unlike certain other people, I respected her grief and kept my distance for the better part of a week, allowing this woman, in her own private way, to come to terms with her terrible irony. I even offered the use of my own personal team of lawyers, hoping that she might sue the owners of that satellite truck because, I don't know about you, but it makes me mad as hell to see a child run down by an inferior network. Speaking through her brother, the young woman declined to initiate a lawsuit or even to press charges. Anyone with the brains of a common gnat would have squeezed those bastards for all they've got, but this simple countrywoman chose instead to shut herself away with nothing but a Bible to ease her terrible pain. It was her right to decide against a lawsuit, but to turn down my generous offer to dramatize her story is an act that borders on madness. It's been rumored that she is motivated by her deeply held religious beliefs and that is why, on this Christmas morning, I am turning to you, her fellow parishioners.

Let me just lay my cards on the table and give it to you straight. You are a poor people. But you don't deserve to be. I've spent some time in this area and have seen your pathetic, ramshackle houses resembling so many piles of firewood. These are places I wouldn't use to store a lawn mower, let alone raise a family. People in our inner-city ghettos are riding around in brand-new Jeeps, yet you walk to church every Sunday, lucky just to have shoes on your feet. But it doesn't have to be that way. Here it is, Christmas Day and your children probably woke to find a kneesock full of twice-chewed gum or a doll made out of used Band-Aids. I'm not putting down handmade gifts, but don't they deserve something better than what you can currently afford to give them?

I'm going to be honest with you people. The truth is that your minister is not just "running late" for this morning's service. He's right outside this building, settled comfortably into the backseat of my car. I'd approached him a few days ago, asking if I might address the congregation. He said, "No sir, you may not." Then I showed him some blueprints drawn up by one of our country's most prestigious architects. They're the plans for your new church because, People, this one is coming down. (Hold for applause.) The bulldozers are arriving first thing tomorrow morning to begin construction of a magnificent temple designed by the same man who brought us the Wasp's Head Convention Center in Houston, Texas. The new steeple will playfully resemble a hypodermic needle. You'll have stainless-steel pews and a burnished concrete altar so big even the Catholics will be jealous.

This new church is a Christmas present. A very expensive Christmas present from me to you with no strings attached. But a new church won't put food in your stomach or pay the doctor bills the next time little Jethro swallows a fistful of thumbtacks. What if I was to tell you that, in return for one small favor, I'd be willing to offer a little help in that direction? Ladies and Gentlemen, this is one year when Santa's definitely coming to town. The question is: Do you welcome him with open arms or turn him away, much like a certain young woman and her devious brother to whom money means nothing?

You know, flying in early this morning, I thought I might offer each of you a brand-new car and a thousand dollars in cash. Now, though, looking out over your kind, sallow faces, I'm thinking of upping that to a brand-new car, a factory-fresh side-by-side refrigerator/freezer, and twelve hundred dollars in cash. Sound good? (Raise eyebrows, establish eye contact.) That's what I promise to give each and every one of you if you can convince this young woman to help me tell her story. Apparently the finer things in life mean nothing to her, and so be it. But is it fair for her to force you, her friends and neighbors, to suffer the same lifestyle?

By refusing to sign my contract and spend an afternoon recounting the facts to me and my topnotch writers, this young woman is ensuring that none of you will ever experience the pleasures that most civilized people take for granted. She'll be saying, "Fine, let their newborn babies die of malnutrition and staph infections." She lost *her* son the hard way and maybe, in her mind, you should, too! Me, I'm more than happy to provide you with a clean and modern building in which to hold their sad little funerals. If, however, you want the money to *prevent* such wasteful, untimely deaths, you'll have to talk it over with your so-called Sister. Maybe *you* can reason with her.

Is this the Christmas your holiday dreams come true, or is it the day you discover just how petty and spiteful one person can truly be? If, like her, you're not interested in money, cars, and appliances, you could still convince her to sign the contract and then donate your rewards to charity. You'd have a pretty hard time finding people less fortunate than yourselves, but if that's your bag, I'd be more than happy to respect it. Giving is what the holiday season is all about. I'm giving you a brand-new church and you don't even have to thank me for it if you don't want to. That's not why I gave it. And if you don't want to repay me by talking some sense into your friend, then I'll just take it on the chin and head on home. I'm just wondering how easy it will be to sleep tonight with your threadbare blankets and Christian ethics knowing that somewhere outside your plastic-paned windows an old crippled woman is begging for coins in some glass-filled gutter because you were too wrapped up in yourself to give her a side-by-side refrigerator/ freezer. Because, let me tell you something, *not* giving is no different than taking. (Good point. Let it sink in.)

I was going to leave you with that thought but, as long as I'm here, let me add a little something else. Even if you refuse to reason with this young woman, I will still produce my holiday special. This, though, will be *my* story, requiring the help of no one. It will be about a small group of so-called evangelical Christians so busy rolling on the floor and beating their tambourines that they've forgotten what Christmas really stands for. It won't have an uplifting seasonal message and may very well send a good twenty million children off to bed thinking that perhaps this God person isn't everything he's cracked up to be, that maybe they're celebrating the birthday of a con artist no different than the stick figures worshipped by the Pygmies or the Moslems. I'm going to write that idea onto a piece of paper (pull out pad, scribble) and hand it to one of my associates just as soon as he returns from his vacation in Bahoorahoo. I'd prefer to do the more compelling story of your young friend, but that, Ladies and Gentlemen, is up to you. It takes time to produce a topnotch holiday special and my people need to get on the stick if we're going to have something ready for next Christmas. Do the catering trucks roll into town early next week, loaded down with cola and mouthwatering pasta salads, free of charge to any shabbily dressed church member wanting to earn good money as an extra? Or do we film an uglier version of the story on some faraway soundstage? One year from today will you be seated on a nice new sofa, watching as this young woman's heart-wrenching miracle is brought to life on your wide-screen TV, or will you be picking the thorns out from between your toes and wondering where you went wrong?

Maybe *you* can let things happen in their own sweet time but me, I can't wait that long. I have a plane to catch early this afternoon, so that leaves you with three hours to hash things over with your young friend. That's three hours *without* commercials, which amounts to two hours and twelve minutes in my time. Your minister has refused to address the topic in his holiday sermon, so he'll be talking about something else. Eventually though, he's going to stop talking and you will have to start thinking. And I would advise you to think carefully. All I'm asking for is a few details. They're little things, details, but they can make all the difference in the world when it comes to fulfilling a dream. Maybe while you're thinking you can entertain a few detailed dreams of your own. I want you to imagine yourselves leaning back against the warm, fragrant upholstery of a brand-new automobile. Your healthy children are still fighting over who got to ride in the front seat but you don't allow that to bother you. In time they'll return their attention to that bounty of toys lying at their feet. Back at the house the ice cubes are eagerly awaiting the kiss of a finely aged bourbon, and there's still enough money in your wallet to make your neighbor jealous. It's Christmas Day, and all is right with the world.

DAVID SEDARIS

Christmas Means Giving

For the first twelve years of our marriage Beth and I happily set the neighborhood standard for comfort and luxury. It was an established fact that we were brighter and more successful but the community seemed to accept our superiority without much complaint and life flowed on the way it should. I used to own a hedge polisher, an electric shovel, and three Rolex gas grills that stood side by side in the backyard. One was for chicken, one for beef, and the third I had specially equipped to steam the oriental pancakes we were always so fond of. When the holidays rolled around I used to rent a moving van and drive into the city, snatching up every bright new extravagance that caught my eye. Our twin sons, Taylor and Weston, could always count on the latest electronic toy or piece of sporting equipment. Beth might receive a riding vacuum cleaner or a couple pair of fur-lined jeans and those were just the stocking stuffers! There were disposable boats, ultrasuede basketballs, pewter knapsacks, and solar-powered card shufflers. I'd buy them shoes and clothes and bucketfuls of jewelry from the finest boutiques and department stores. Far be it from me to snoop around for a bargain or discount. I always paid top dollar, thinking that those foot-long price tags really *meant* something about Christmas. After opening our gifts we'd sit down to a sumptuous banquet, feasting on every imaginable variety of meat and pudding. When one of us got full and felt uncomfortable, we'd stick a silver wand down our throats, throw up, and start eating all over again. In effect, we weren't much different from anyone else. Christmas was a season of bounty and, to the outside world, we were just about the most bountiful people anyone could think of. We thought we were happy but that all changed on one crisp Thanksgiving day shortly after the Cottinghams arrived.

If my memory serves me correctly, the Cottinghams were trouble from the very first moment they moved in next door. Doug, Nancy, and their unattractive eight-year-old daughter, Eileen, were exceedingly envious and greedy people. Their place was a little smaller than ours but it made sense, seeing as there were four of us and only three of them. Still though, something about the size of our house so bothered them that they hadn't even unpacked the first suitcase before starting construction on an indoor skating rink and a three-thousand-square-foot pavilion where Doug could show off his collection of pre-Columbian sofa beds. Because we felt like doing so, Beth and I then began construction on an indoor soccer field and a five-thousand-square-foot rotunda where I could comfortably display *my* collection of pre-*pre*-Columbian sofa beds. Doug would tell all the neighbors I'd stolen the idea from him but I'd been thinking about pre-pre-Columbian sofa beds long before the Cottinghams pulled into town. They just had to cause trouble, no matter what the cost. When Beth and I built a seven-screen multiplex theater they had to go and build themselves a *twelve*-screener. This went on and on and, to make a long story short, within a year's time neither one of us had much of a yard. The two houses now butted right up against each other and we blocked out the west-side windows so that we wouldn't have to look into their gaudy fitness center or second-story rifle range.

Despite their competitive nature, Beth and I tried our best to be neighborly and occasionally invite them over for rooftop barbecues and so forth. I'd attempt to make adult conversation, saying something like "I just paid eight thousand dollars for a pair of sandals that don't even fit me." Doug would counter, saying that he himself had just paid ten thousand for a single flip-flop he wouldn't wear even if it *did* fit him. He was always very combative that way. If it cost you seventy thousand dollars to have a cavity filled, you could bet your boots it cost him at least a hundred and twenty-five thousand. I suffered his company for the better part of a year until one November evening when we got into a spat over which family sent out the most meaningful Christmas card. Beth and I normally hired a noted photographer to snap a portrait of the entire family surrounded by the gifts we had received the year before. Inside the card would be the price of these gifts along with the message "Christmas Means Giving." The Cottinghams favored *their* card, which consisted of a Xeroxed copy of Doug and Nancy's stock portfolio. I said that while it is all very well and good to *have* money, their card said nothing about the way they *spent* money. Like our card said, Christmas means giving and even if he were to gussy up his stock report with a couple of press-on candy canes it would still fail to send the proper holiday message. The conversation grew quite heated and some punches were thrown between the wives. We'd all had a few drinks and by the time the Cottinghams left our house it was generally assumed that our friendship was over. I dwelled upon the incident for a day or two and then turned my attention toward the approaching holidays.

We'd just finished another of our gut-busting Thanksgiving dinners and Beth, the boys, and I were watching a bullfight on TV. We could watch whatever we wanted back then because we still had our satellite dish. Juan Carlos Ponce de Velasquez had just been gored something fierce and we were all acting pretty excited about it when the doorbell rang. I figured one of the boys had ordered a pizza and opened the door surprised to find a foul-smelling beggar. He was a thin, barefooted man with pepperoni-sized scabs on his legs and an unkempt beard smeared with several different varieties of jam. I sensed it was the jam we'd thrown into the garbage the night before and one look at our overturned trash can told me I was right. This had me pretty ticked off but before I could say anything about it, the old bum pulled out a coffee mug and started whining for money.

When Beth asked who was at the door I called out, "Code Blue," which was our secret signal that one of us should release the hounds. We had two of them back then, big Dobermans named Butterscotch and Mr. Lewis. Beth tried to summon them from the dining room but, having gorged themselves on turkey and stuffing, it was all they could do to lift their heads and vomit. Seeing as they were laid up, I got down on my hands and knees and bit the guy myself. Maybe it was the bullfight but, for whatever reason, I had a sudden taste for blood. My teeth barely broke the skin but that was all it took to send the old coot hobbling over to the Cottinghams' place. I watched him pound upon their door, knowing full well what would happen when he told competitive Doug Copy Cat that I'd given him one measly bite on the calf. Beth called me into the house for one reason or another and when I returned to the door a few minutes later, I saw Helvetica, the Cottinghams' maid, taking a photograph of Doug, Nancy, and Eileen handing the tramp a one-dollar bill.

I knew something was up and, sure enough, two weeks later I came to find that exact same snapshot on the Cottinghams' Christmas card along with the words "Christmas means giving." That had always been *our* slogan and here he'd stolen it, twisting the message in an attempt to make us appear selfish. It had never been our way to give to others but I started having second thoughts when I noticed the phenomenal response the Cottinghams received on the basis of their Christmas card. Suddenly they were all anyone was talking about. Walk into any holiday party and you'd hear, "Did you see it? I think it's positively enchanting. Here these people donated money to an absolute stranger! Can you beat that? A whole dollar they gave to this vagrant person with absolutely nothing to his name. If you ask me, those Cottinghams are a couple of very brave and generous people."

Doug would probably say that I unfairly stole his idea when I myself became a generous person but this was not the case. I'd been thinking of being generous long before he showed up on the scene and, besides that, if he could illegally pinch my holiday slogan, why couldn't I casually borrow a concept that had been around for a good ten years? When I first told people that I had given two dollars to the Inner City Headache Fund they turned away as if they didn't believe me. Then I actually *did* give two dollars to the Headache Fund and boy, did things ever change once I started flashing around that canceled check! Generosity can actually make people feel quite uncomfortable if you talk about it enough. I don't mean the bad "boring uncomfortable" but something much richer. If practiced correctly, generosity can induce feelings of shame, inadequacy, and even envy, to name just a few. The most important thing is that you keep some written or visual proof of your donation, otherwise there's really no point in giving to charity. Doug Cottingham would say I took that line from him but I'm pretty sure I read it in a tax manual.

I carried my canceled check to all the important holiday parties but people lost interest shortly after New Year's Eve. The seasons passed and I forgot all about my generosity until the following Thanksgiving, when the old tramp returned to our neighborhood. He must have remembered the previous year's bite to the leg and, as a result, he was just about to pass us by when we called him in for a good dose of benevolence. First we videotaped him eating a palmful of leftover stuffing and then I had Beth snap a picture as I handed the geezer a VCR. It was an old top-loading Betamax but put a new cord on it and I'm sure it would have worked just fine. We watched then as he strapped it on his back and headed next door to continue his begging. The sight of that VCR was all it took for that skunk Doug Cottingham, who stepped into his house and returned to present the old codger with an eight-track tape deck and, oh, once again their maid was on hand to take a picture of it. We then called the tramp over to our house and gave him a year-old blow-dryer. The Cottinghams responded with a toaster oven. Within an hour we had advanced to pool tables and StairMasters. Doug gave him a golf cart and I gave him my satellite dish. This accelerated until any fool could see exactly where it was heading. Handing over the keys to his custom-built motorized travel sauna, Doug Cottingham gave me a look that seemed to say, "Top *that*, Neighbor!" Beth and I had seen that look before and we hated it. I could have easily topped his travel sauna but we were running low on film and thought it best to cut to the chase. Why needlessly escalate when we all knew what was most important? After a brief conference, Beth and I called the tramp back over and asked which he liked better, young boys or young girls. Much to our delight he said that girls were too much of a headache but that he'd had some fun with boys before his last visit to our local state penitentiary. That said, we gave him our ten-year-old sons, Taylor and Weston. Top that, Neighbor! You should have seen the look on Doug Cottingham's face! That year's Christmas card was the most meaningful to date. It pictured our sons' tearful good-bye along with the message "Christmas means giving until it hurts."

We were the toast of the neighborhood that holiday season, back on top where we belonged. Beth and I were *the* couple to have at any cocktail party or informal tree trimming.

"Where are those supergenerous people with that delightful Christmas card?" someone would ask, and the host would point in our direction while the Cottinghams bitterly gritted their teeth. As a last-ditch effort to better their names they donated their horse-faced daughter, Eileen, to a crew of needy pirates but anyone in the know could see it as the desperate gesture it really was. Once again we were the ones everyone wanted to be with and the warm glow of their admiration carried us through the holiday season. We received a second helping of awe early the following summer when the boys were discovered dead in what used to be Doug Cottingham's motorized travel sauna. The neighbors all wanted to send flowers but we said we'd prefer them to make a donation in our name to the National Sauna Advisory Board or the Sex Offenders Defense Fund. This was a good move and soon we had established ourselves as "Christlike." The Cottinghams were, of course, furious and immediately set to work on their tired game of one-upsmanship. It was most likely the only thing they thought about but we didn't lose any sleep over it.

For that year's holiday cards we had settled on the theme "Christmas means giving until it bleeds." Shortly after Thanksgiving Beth and I had visited our local blood bank, where we nearly drained our bodies' precious accounts. Pale and dizzy from our efforts, it was all we could do to lift a hand and wave to one another from our respective gurneys. We recovered in time and were just sealing our envelopes when the postman delivered our neighbors' holiday card, which read "Christmas means giving of yourself." The cover pictured Doug lying outstretched upon an operating table as a team of surgeons busily, studiously, removed his glistening Cottingham lung. Inside the card was a photograph of the organ's recipient, a haggard coal miner holding a sign that read "Douglas Cottingham saved my life."

How dare he! Beth and I had practically invented the theme of medical generosity and it drove us mad, that smug, superior expression seeping from beneath our neighbor's surgical mask. Any long-married couple can, in times of crisis, communicate without speaking. This fact was illustrated as my wife and I wordlessly leapt into action. Throwing down her half-sealed envelope, Beth called the hospital while I contacted a photographer from our car phone. Arrangements were made and before the night was over I had donated both my eyes, a lung, one of my kidneys, and several important veins surrounding my heart. Having an unnatural attachment to her internal organs, Beth surrendered her scalp, her teeth, her right leg, and both breasts. It wasn't until after her surgery that we realized my wife's contributions were nontransferable, but by that time it was too late to sew them back on. She gave the scalp to a startled cancer patient, made a keepsake necklace of her teeth, and brought the leg and breasts to the animal shelter, where they were hand-fed to a litter of starving Border collies. That made the local evening news and once again the Cottinghams were green with envy over our good fortune. Donating organs to humans was one thing, but the community went wild over what Beth had done for those poor abandoned puppies. At each and every holiday party our hosts would beg my wife to shake their dog's hand or pass a blessing over the shell of their ailing tortoise. The coal-mining recipient of Doug Cottingham's lung had died when his cigarette set fire to the sheets and bandages covering his chest and now their name was practically worthless.

We were at the Hepplewhites' Christmas Eve party when I overheard Beth whisper, "That Doug Cottingham couldn't even donate a decent lung!" She laughed then, long and hard, and I placed my hand upon her shoulder, feeling the gentle bite of her keepsake necklace. I was no doubt drawing a good deal of attention myself, but this was Beth's night and I gave it to her freely because I was such a generous person. We were a team, she and I, and while I couldn't see the way people were looking at us, I could feel it just as surely as I sensed the warmth cast off by the Hepplewhites' roaring fire.

There would be other Christmases, but I think Beth and I both knew that this one was special. In a year's time we would give away the house, our money, and what remained of our possessions. After scouting around for the right neighborhood, we would move into a village of cardboard boxes located beneath the Ragsdale Cloverleaf. The Cottinghams, true to their nature, would move into a smaller box next door. The begging would go relatively well during the holiday season but come deep winter things would get hard and we'd be visited by wave after wave of sorrow and disease. Beth would die after a long, sad struggle with tuberculosis but not until after Doug Cottingham and his wife had been killed by pneumonia. I'd try not to let it bother me that they had died first but in truth I would have a very difficult time dealing with it. Whenever my jealousy would get the best of me I would reflect back upon that perfect Christmas Eve at the Hepplewhites'. Shuddering beneath my blanket of damp newspapers, I'd try to recall the comforting sound of Beth's carefree laughter and picture her raw head thrown back in merriment, those bright, gleaming gums reflecting the light of a crystal chandelier. With luck, the memory of our love and generosity would lull me toward a profound and heavy sleep that would last until morning.

Dinah,
the Christmas Whore

It was my father's belief that nothing built character better than an after-school job. He himself had peddled newspapers and delivered groceries by bobsled, and look at him! My older sister, Lisa, and I decided that if hard work had forged *his* character, we wanted nothing to do with it. "Thanks but no thanks," we said.

As an added incentive, he cut off our allowance, and within a few weeks Lisa and I were both working in cafeterias. I washed dishes at the Piccadilly while Lisa manned the steam tables at K&W. Situated in Raleigh's first indoor shopping center, her cafeteria was a clubhouse for the local senior citizens who might spend an entire afternoon huddled over a single serving of rice pudding. The K&W was past its prime, whereas my cafeteria was located in the sparkling new Crabtree Valley, a former swamp that made her mall look like a dusty tribal marketplace. The Piccadilly had red velvet walls and a dining room lit by artificial torches. A suit of armor marked the entrance to this culinary castle where, we were told, the customer was always king.

As a dishwasher, I spent my shifts yanking trays off a conveyor belt and feeding their contents into an enormous, foul-mouthed machine that roared and spat until its charges, free of congealed fat and gravy, came steaming out the other end, fogging my glasses and filling the air with the harsh smell of chlorine.

I didn't care for the heat or the noise, but other than that, I enjoyed my job. The work kept my hands busy but left my mind free to concentrate on more important matters. Sometimes I would study from the list of irregular Spanish verbs I kept posted over the sink, but most often I found myself fantasizing about a career in television. It was my dream to create and star in a program called "Socrates and Company," in which I would travel from place to place accompanied by a brilliant and loyal proboscis monkey. Socrates and I wouldn't go looking for trouble, but week after week it would manage to find us. "The eyes, Socrates, go for the eyes," I'd yell during one of our many fight scenes.

Maybe in Santa Fe I'd be hit over the head by a heavy jug and lose my memory. Somewhere in Utah Socrates might discover a satchel of valuable coins or befriend someone wearing a turban, but at the end of every show we would realize that true happiness often lies where you very least expect it. It might arrive in the form of a gentle breeze or a handful of peanuts, but when it came, we would seize it with our own brand of folksy wisdom. I'd planned it so that the final moments of each episode would find Socrates and me standing before a brilliant sunset as I reminded both my friend and the viewing audience of the lesson I had learned. "It suddenly occurred to me that there are things far more valuable than gold," I might say, watching a hawk glide high above a violet butte. Plotting the episodes was no more difficult than sorting the silverware; the hard part was thinking up the all-important revelation. "It suddenly occurred to me that . . ." That what? Things hardly ever occurred to me. It might occasionally strike me that I'd broken a glass or filled the machine with too much detergent, but the larger issues tended to elude me.

Like several of the other local cafeterias, the Piccadilly often hired former convicts whose jobs were arranged through parole officers and work-release programs. During my downtime I often hung around their area of the kitchen, hoping that in listening to these felons, something profound might reveal itself. "It suddenly occurred to me that we are all held captive in that prison known as the human mind," I would muse, or "It suddenly occurred to me that freedom was perhaps the greatest gift of all." I'd hoped to crack these people like nuts, sifting through their brains and coming away with the lessons garnered by a lifetime of regret. Unfortunately, having spent the better part of their lives behind bars, the men and women I worked with seemed to have learned nothing except how to get out of doing their jobs.

Kettles boiled over and steaks were routinely left to blacken on the grill as my coworkers crept off to the stockroom to smoke and play cards or sometimes have sex. "It suddenly occurred to me that people are lazy," my reflective TV voice would say. This was hardly a major news flash, and as a closing statement, it would undoubtedly fail to warm the hearts of my television audience — who, by their very definition, were probably not too active themselves. No, my message needed to be upbeat and spiritually rewarding. *Joy*, I'd think, whacking the dirty plates against the edge of the slop can. *What brings people joy?*

As Christmas approached, I found my valuable fantasy time cut in half. The mall was crazy now with hungry shoppers, and every three minutes I had the assistant manager on my back hollering for more coffee cups and vegetable bowls. The holiday customers formed a loud and steady line that reached past the coat of arms all the way to the suit of armor at the front door. They wore cheerful Santas pinned to their baubled sweatshirts and carried oversized bags laden with power tools and assorted cheeses bought as gifts for friends and relatives. It made me sad and desperate to see so many people, strangers whose sheer numbers eroded the sense of importance I was working so hard to invent. Where did they come from, and why couldn't they just go home? I might swipe their trays off the belt without once wondering who these people were and why they hadn't bothered to finish their breaded cutlets. They meant nothing to me, and watching them move down the line toward the cashier, it became apparent that the feeling was mutual. They wouldn't even remember the meal, much less the person who had provided them with their piping hot tray. How was it that I was important and they were not? There had to be something that separated us.

I had always looked forward to Christmas, but now my enthusiasm struck me as cheap and common. Leaving the cafeteria after work, I would see even more people, swarming out of the shops and restaurants like bees from a burning hive. Here were the young couples in their stocking caps and the families clustered beside the fountain, each with its lists and marked envelopes of money. It was no wonder the Chinese people couldn't tell them apart. They were sheep, stupid animals programmed by nature to mate and graze and bleat out their wishes to the obese, retired school principal who sat on his ass in the mall's sorry-looking North Pole.

My animosity was getting the best of me until I saw in their behavior a solution to my troubling identity crisis. Let them have their rolls of gift wrap and gaudy, personalized stockings: if it meant something to them, I wanted nothing to do with it. This year I would be the one *without* the shopping bags, the one wearing black in protest of their thoughtless commercialism. My very avoidance would set me apart and cause these people to question themselves in ways that would surely pain them. "Who *are* we?" they'd ask, plucking the ornaments off their trees. "What have we become and why can't we be more like that somber fellow who washes dishes down at the Piccadilly cafeteria?"

My boycott had a practical edge, as this year I wasn't expecting to receive much of anything. In an effort to save money, my family had decided to try something new and draw names. This cruel lottery left my fate in the hands of Lisa, whose idea of a decent gift was a six-pack of flashlight batteries or a scented candle in the shape of a toadstool. Patently, joyfully normal, Lisa was the embodiment of everything I found depressing. Nothing set her apart from the thousands of other girls I saw each day, but this fact did not disturb her in the least. In her desire to be typical, my sister had succeeded with flying, muted colors. Unlike me, she would never entertain deep thoughts or travel to distant lands in the company of a long-nosed proboscis monkey. None of them would. Along with everyone else, she had traded her soul in exchange for a stocking stuffer and now would have to suffer the consequences.

As the holiday season advanced, so did my impatience. Four days before Christmas we were seated in the dining room, celebrating Lisa's eighteenth birthday, when she received a phone call from what sounded like a full-grown woman with a mouth full of gravel. When I asked who was calling, the woman hesitated before identifying herself as "a friend. I'm a goddamned friend, all right?" This caught my attention because, to my knowledge, my sister had no adult friends, goddamned or otherwise. I handed her the phone and watched as she carried it out into the carport, stretching the cord to its limit. It was a forbidden act, and because I felt like causing some trouble, I told on her. "Dad, Lisa carried the receiver outside and now it looks like the phone is going to spring off the wall."

He started out of his chair before my mother said, "Leave her alone, for God's sake, it's her birthday. If the phone breaks, I'll buy you another one for Christmas." She gave me a look usually reserved for eight-legged creatures found living beneath the kitchen sink. "You always have to stir the turd, don't you?"

"But she's talking to a *woman!*" I said.

My mother crushed her cigarette into her plate. "Big deal, so are you."

Lisa returned to the table in a hurried, agitated state, asking my parents if she might use the station wagon. "David and I should be back in an hour or so," she said, grabbing our coats from the front-hall closet.

"David who?" I asked. "This David's not going anywhere." I'd hoped to spend the evening in my bedroom, working on the pastel portrait of Socrates I planned to quietly give myself as an anti-Christmas present. We stood negotiating in the dark driveway until I agreed to join her, no questions asked, in exchange for three dollars and unlimited use of her new hair dryer. Having settled that, we got into the car and drove past the brightly decorated homes of north Raleigh. Normally, Lisa demanded strict control of the radio. At the sight of my fingers approaching the dial, she would smack my hand and threaten to toss me out of the car, but tonight she gave me no grief, failing to complain even when I settled on a local talk show devoted to the theme of high-school basketball. I couldn't stand basketball and only tuned in to get a rise out of her. "How about those Spartans," I said, nudging her in the shoulder. "You think they've got what it takes to defeat the Imps and move on to the city championship?"

"Whatever. I don't know. Maybe."

Something had clearly placed her beyond my reach, and it drove me wild with something that felt very much like jealousy. "What? Are we going to meet up with the mother of your boyfriend? How much do you have to pay her to allow him to go out with you? You have a boyfriend, is that it?"

She ignored my questions, quietly muttering to herself as she drove us past the capitol building and into a defeated neighborhood where the porches sagged and a majority of the windows sported sheets and towels rather than curtains. People got knifed in places like this, I heard about it all the time on my radio call-in shows. Had my father been driving, we would have locked all the doors and ignored the stop signs, speeding through the area as quickly as possible because that's what smart people did.

"All right, then." Lisa pulled over and parked behind a van whose owner stood examining his flattened tire with a flashlight. "Things might get a little rough up there, so just do what I tell you and hopefully no one will get hurt." She flipped her hair over her shoulder and stepped out of the car, kicking aside the cans and bottles that lined the curb. My sister meant business, whatever it was, and in that instant she appeared beautiful and exotic and dangerously stupid. LOCAL TEENS SLAIN FOR SPORT the headlines would read. HOLIDAY HIJINKS END IN HOMICIDE.

"Maybe someone should wait with the car," I whispered, but she was beyond reason, charging up the street in her sensible shoes with a rugged, determined gait. There was no fumbling for a street address or doorbell; Lisa seemed to know exactly where she was going. I followed her into a dark vestibule and up a flight of stairs, where without even bothering to knock, she threw open an unlocked door and stormed into a filthy, overheated room that smelled of stale smoke, sour milk, and seriously dirty laundry — three odors that, once combined, can peel the paint off walls.

This was a place where bad things happened to people who clearly deserved nothing but the worst. The stained carpet was littered with cigarette butts and clotted, dust-covered flypaper hung from the ceiling like beaded curtains. In the far corner of the room, a man stood beside an overturned coffee table, illuminated by a shadeless lamp that broadcast his shadow, huge and menacing, against the grimy wall. He was dressed casually in briefs and a soiled T-shirt and had thin, hairless legs the color and pebbled texture of a store-bought chicken.

We had obviously interrupted some rite of unhappiness, something that involved shouting obscenities while pounding upon a locked door with a white-tasseled loafer. The activity consumed him so completely that it took the man a few moments to register our presence. Squinting in our direction, he dropped the shoe and steadied himself against the mantel.

"Why if it isn't Lisa Fucking Sedaris. I should have known that bitch would call a fucking bitch like you."

I would have been less shocked had a seal called my sister by name. How was it that she knew this man? Staggeringly drunk, the wasted, boozy Popeye charged in our direction, and Lisa rushed to meet him. I watched then, cringing, as she caught him by the neck, throwing him down against the coffee table before gathering her fists and dancing in a tight circle, thoroughly prepared to take on any hidden comers. It was as if she had spent a lifetime dressed in a black *gi*, breaking two-by-fours with her bare hands in preparation for this moment. She never faltered or cried out for help, just gave him a few swift kicks in the ribs and proceeded to carry out her mission.

"I ain't done nothing," the man moaned, turning to me with his bloodshot eyes. "You there, tell that bitch I hadn't done nothing."

"I beg your pardon?" I inched toward the door. "Oh, golly, I don't know what to tell you. I'm just, you know, I just came along for the ride."

"Guard him!" Lisa yelled.

Guard him how? Who did she think I was? "Don't leave me," I cried, but she had already gone, and suddenly I was alone with this shattered man, who massaged his chest and begged me to fetch his cigarettes off the sofa.

"Go on, boy, get 'em. Fucking bitches. Lord Jesus, I'm in pain."

I heard my sister's voice and looked up to see her fleeing the back room, dragging behind her a clownish, tear-stained woman of an indeterminate age. Her face was lined and puffy. The thick, fat, mottled body had a lot of mileage on it, but her clothing was unseasonable and absurdly youthful. While my mother's crowd favored holiday maxiskirts and turquoise squash-blossom necklaces, this woman had attempted to offset the ravages of time with denim hot pants and a matching vest that, fastened together by a cross-hatching system of rawhide laces, afforded an unfortunate view of her sagging, ponderous breasts.

"Out!" Lisa shouted. "Hurry, now, step on it!"

I was way ahead of her.

"My shoes and, oh, I better take a jacket," the woman said. "And while I'm at it . . ." Her voice faded as I raced down the stairs, past the other equally dark and volatile doorways where people fought over the noise of their screeching televisions. I was out on the street, panting for breath and wondering how many times my sister would be stabbed or bludgeoned when I heard the screen door slam and saw Lisa appear on the front porch. She paused on the stoop, waiting as the woman put on a jacket and stuffed her feet into a pair of shoes that, in their bulk and color, resembled a matching set of paint cans. Instructed once again to run, her friend proceeded to totter down the street on what amounted to a pair of stilts. It was an awkward, useless style of walking, and with each step she ran her fingers through the air as if she were playing a piano.

Two young men passed down the sidewalk carrying a mattress, and one of them turned to yell, "Get that ho off the street!"

Had we been in a richer or poorer neighborhood, I might have searched the ground for a gardening tool, fearful that once again I might step on the thing and split my lip with the handle. *Ho.* I'd heard that word bandied about by the cooks at work, who leered and snickered much like the young men with their mattress. It took me a second to realize that they were referring either to Lisa or to her friend, who was squatting to examine a hole in her fishnet stockings. A whore. Of the two possible nominees, the friend seemed the more likely candidate. At the mention of the word, she had lifted her head and given a little wave. This woman was the real thing, and I studied her, my breath shallow and visible in the cold, dark air. Like a heroin addict or a mass murderer, a prostitute was, to me, more exotic than any celebrity could ever hope to be. You'd see them downtown after dark, sticking their hatchety faces into the windows of idling cars. "Hey there, Flossie, what do you charge for a lube job," my father would shout. I always wanted him to pull over so we could get a better look, but having made his little comment, he'd roll up the window and speed off, chuckling.

"Dinah, this is David. David, Dinah." Lisa made the introductions after we'd settled ourselves into the car. Apparently, the two of them worked together at the K&W and had come to know each other quite well.

"Oh, that Gene is a real hothead," Dinah said. "He's possessive, like I told you, but, Lord, that man just can't help himself from loving me. Maybe we'll just drive around the block a few times and give him a chance to cool off." She lit a cigarette and dropped it, lowering her high, teased head of hair before sighing, "Oh, well, it won't be the first car I've set fire to."

"Found it!" Lisa held the cigarette to her lips and inhaled deeply, releasing the smoke through her nostrils. A beginner would have gagged, but she puffed away like a withered old pro. What other tricks had she learned recently? Was there a packet of heroin tucked inside her pocket? Had she taken to throwing knives or shooting pool while the rest of us were asleep in our beds? She stared thoughtfully at the street before asking, "Dinah, are you drunk?"

"Yes, ma'am, I am," the woman answered. "I surely am."

"And Gene was drunk, too, am I wrong?"

"A little bit drunk," Dinah said. "But that's his way. We like to get drunk in the winter when there's nothing else to do."

"And is that good for your work-release program? Is getting drunk and having fistfights something that's going to keep you out of trouble?"

"It wasn't nothing but horseplay. It got out of hand is all."

Lisa didn't seem to mind making the woman uncomfortable. "You told me yesterday at the steam table that you were ready to break it off with that sorry little bastard and work your way up to carving. A person's got to have steady hands if she wants to carve meat all day, don't you know that?"

Dinah snapped. "I can't remember everything I said at the goddamned steam table. Hell's bells, girl, I never would have called if I'd known you was going to hassle me half to death. Turn around, now, I want to go home."

"Oh, I'm taking you home all right," Lisa said.

The sorry neighborhood receded into the distance, and Dinah turned in her seat, squinting until her eyes were completely shut, and she fell asleep.

"Mom, this is Dinah. Dinah, this is my mother."

"Oh, thank goodness," my mother said, helping our guest out of her shoddy rabbit jacket. "For a moment there, I was afraid you were one of those damned carolers. I wasn't expecting company, so you'll have to excuse the way I look."

The way *she* looked? Dinah's mascara had smeared, causing her to resemble a ridiculously costumed panda, and here my mother was apologizing for the way *she* looked? I took her aside for a moment.

"Whore," I whispered. "That lady is a whore." I'm not certain what reaction I was after, but shock would have done quite nicely.

Instead, my mother said, "Well, then, we should probably offer her a drink." She left me standing in the dining room listening as she presented the woman with a long list of options delivered in alphabetical order. "We've got beer, bourbon, gin, ouzo, rum, scotch, vodka, whiskey, wine, and some thick yellow something or other in an unmarked bottle."

When Dinah spilled her cocktail onto the clean holiday tablecloth, my mother apologized as though it had been her fault for filling the glass too high. "I tend to do that sometimes. Here, let me get you another."

Hearing a fresh, slurred voice in the house, my brother and sisters rushed from their rooms and gathered to examine Lisa's friend, who clearly cherished the attention. "Angels," Dinah said. "You're a pack of goddamned angels." She was surrounded by admirers, and her eyes brightened with each question or comment.

"Which do you like better," my sister Amy asked, "spending the night with strange guys or working in a cafeteria? What were the prison guards *really* like? Do you ever carry a weapon? How much do you charge if somebody just wants a spanking?"

"One at a time, one at a time," my mother said. "Give her a second to answer."

Tiffany tried on Dinah's shoes while Gretchen modeled her jacket. Birthday cake was offered and candles were lit. My six-year-old brother emptied ashtrays, blushing with pride when Dinah complimented him on his efficiency. "This one here ought to be working down at the cafeteria," she said. "He's got the arms of a busboy and eyes like an assistant manager. Nothing slips by you, does it, sweetheart? Let's see if he can freshen up an old lady's drink."

Woken by the noise, my father wandered up from the basement, where he'd been sitting in his underwear, drowsing in front of the television. His approach generally marked the end of the party. "What the hell are you doing in here at two o'clock in the morning?" he'd shout. It was his habit to add anywhere from three to four hours to the actual time in order to strengthen the charge of disorderly conduct. The sun could still be shining, and he'd claim it was midnight. Point to the clock and he'd only throw up his hands to say, "Bullshit! Go to bed."

This evening he was in a particularly foul mood and announced his arrival well before entering the room. "What are you, tap-dancing up there? You want to put on a show, do you? Well, the theater's closed for the night. Take your act on the road; it's four o'clock in the morning, goddamnit."

We turned instinctively to our mother. "Don't come into the kitchen," she called. "We don't want you to see your . . . Christmas present."

"My present? Really?" His voice softened to a mew. "Carry on, then."

We listened to his footsteps as he padded down the hallway to his room and then we covered our mouths, laughing until our sight was watery. Swallows of cake revisited our throats, and our faces, reflected in the dark windows, were flushed and vibrant.

Every gathering has its moment. As an adult, I distract myself by trying to identify it, dreading the inevitable downswing that is sure to follow. The guests will repeat themselves one too many times, or you'll run out of dope or liquor and realize that it was all you ever had in common. At the time, though, I still believed that such a warm and heady feeling might last forever and that in embracing it fully, I might approximate the same wistful feeling adults found in their second round of drinks. I had hated Lisa, felt jealous of her secret life, and now, over my clotted mug of hot chocolate, I felt for her a great pride. Up and down our street the houses were decorated with plywood angels and mangers framed in colored bulbs. Over on Coronado someone had lashed speakers to his trees, broadcasting carols over the candy-cane forest he'd planted beside his driveway. Our neighbors would rise early and visit the malls, snatching up gift-wrapped DustBusters and the pom-pommed socks used to protect the heads of golf clubs. Christmas would arrive and we, the people of this country, would gather around identical trees, voicing our pleasure with worn clichés. Turkeys would roast to a hard, shellacked finish. Hams would be crosshatched with x's and glazed with fruit — and it was fine by me. Were I to receive a riding vacuum cleaner or even a wizened proboscis monkey, it wouldn't please me half as much as knowing we were the only family in the neighborhood with a prostitute in our kitchen. From this moment on, the phrase "Ho, ho, ho" would take on a whole different meaning; and I, along with the rest of my family, could appreciate it in our own clannish way. It suddenly occurred to me. Just like that.

Jesus Shaves

"And what does one do on the fourteenth of July? Does one celebrate Bastille Day?"

It was my second month of French class, and the teacher was leading us in an exercise designed to promote the use of *one*, our latest personal pronoun.

"Might one sing on Bastille Day?" she asked. "Might one dance in the streets? Somebody give me an answer."

Printed in our textbooks was a list of major holidays accompanied by a scattered arrangement of photographs depicting French people in the act of celebration. The object of the lesson was to match the holiday with the corresponding picture. It was simple enough but seemed an exercise better suited to the use of the pronoun *they*. I didn't know about the rest of the class, but when Bastille Day eventually rolled around, I planned to stay home and clean my oven.

Normally, when working from the book, it was my habit to tune out my fellow students and scout ahead, concentrating on the question I'd calculated might fall to me, but this afternoon we were veering from the usual format. Questions were answered on a volunteer basis, and I was able to sit back and relax, confident that the same few students would do most of the talking. Today's discussion was dominated by an Italian nanny, two chatty Poles, and a pouty, plump Moroccan woman who had grown up speaking French and had enrolled in the class hoping to improve her spelling. She'd covered these lessons back in the third grade and took every opportunity to demonstrate her superiority. A question would be asked, and she'd race to give the answer, behaving as though this were a game show and, if quick enough, she might go home with a tropical vacation or a side-by-side refrigerator/freezer. A transfer student, by the end of her first day she'd raised her hand so many times that her shoulder had given out. Now she just leaned back and shouted out the answers, her bronzed arms folded across her chest like some great grammar genie.

We'd finished discussing Bastille Day, and the teacher had moved on to Easter, which was represented in our textbooks by a black-and-white photograph of a chocolate bell lying upon a bed of palm fronds.

"And what does one do on Easter?" she asked. "Would anyone like to tell us?"

The Italian nanny was attempting to answer when the Moroccan student interrupted, shouting, "Excuse me, but what's an Easter?"

It would seem that despite having grown up in a Muslim country, she would have heard it mentioned once or twice, but no. "I mean it," she said. "I have no idea what you people are talking about."

Our teacher then called upon the rest of us to explain.

The Poles led the charge to the best of their ability. "It is," said one, "a party for the little boy of God who call his self Jesus and . . ." She faltered and her fellow countryman came to her aid.

"He call his self Jesus and then he die one day on two . . . morsels of . . . lumber."

The rest of the class jumped in, offering bits of information that would have given the pope an aneurysm.

"He die one day and then he go above of my head to live with your father."

"He weared of himself the long hair and after he die, the first day he come back here for to say hello to the peoples."

"He nice, the Jesus."

"He make the good things, and on the Easter we be sad because somebody makes him dead today."

Part of the problem had to do with vocabulary. Simple nouns such as *cross* and *resurrection* were beyond our grasp, let alone such complicated reflexive phrases as "to give of yourself your only begotten son." Faced with the challenge of explaining the cornerstone of Christianity, we did what any self-respecting group of people might do. We talked about food instead.

"Easter is a party for to eat of the lamb," the Italian nanny explained. "One too may eat of the chocolate."

"And who brings the chocolate?" the teacher asked.

I knew the word, so I raised my hand, saying, "The rabbit of Easter. He bring of the chocolate."

"A rabbit?" The teacher, assuming I'd used the wrong word, positioned her index fingers on top of her head, wriggling them as though they were ears. "You mean one of these? A *rabbit* rabbit?"

"Well, sure," I said. "He come in the night when one sleep on a bed. With a hand he have a basket and foods."

The teacher sighed and shook her head. As far as she was concerned, I had just explained everything that was wrong with my country. "No, no," she said. "Here in France the chocolate is brought by a big bell that flies in from Rome."

I called for a time-out. "But how do the bell know where you live?"

"Well," she said, "how does a rabbit?"

It was a decent point, but at least a rabbit has eyes. That's a start. Rabbits move from place to place, while most bells can only go back and forth — and they can't even do that on their own power. On top of that, the Easter Bunny has character. He's someone you'd like to meet and shake hands with. A bell has all the personality of a cast-iron skillet. It's like saying that come Christmas, a magic dustpan flies in from the North Pole, led by eight flying cinder blocks. Who wants to stay up all night so they can see a bell? And why fly one in from Rome when they've got more bells than they know what to do with right here in Paris? That's the most implausible aspect of the whole story, as there's no way the bells of France would allow a foreign worker to fly in and take their jobs. That Roman bell would be lucky to get work cleaning up after a French bell's dog — and even then he'd need papers. It just didn't add up.

Nothing we said was of any help to the Moroccan student. A dead man with long hair supposedly living with her father, a leg of lamb served with palm fronds and chocolate; equally confused and disgusted, she shrugged her massive shoulders and turned her attention back to the comic book she kept hidden beneath her binder.

I wondered then if, without the language barrier, my classmates and I could have done a better job making sense of Christianity, an idea that sounds pretty far-fetched to begin with.

In communicating any religious belief, the operative word is *faith*, a concept illustrated by our very presence in that classroom. Why bother struggling with the grammar lessons of a six-year-old if each of us didn't believe that, against all reason, we might eventually improve? If I could hope to one day carry on a fluent conversation, it was a relatively short leap to believing that a rabbit might visit my home in the middle of the night, leaving behind a handful of chocolate kisses and a carton of menthol cigarettes. So why stop there? If I could believe in myself, why not give other improbabilities the benefit of the doubt? I told myself that despite her past behavior, my teacher was a kind and loving person who had only my best interests at heart. I accepted the idea that an omniscient God had cast me in his own image and that he watched over me and guided me from one place to the next. The Virgin Birth, the Resurrection, and the countless miracles — my heart expanded to encompass all the wonders and possibilities of the universe.

A bell, though — that's fucked up.

Us and Them

When my family first moved to North Carolina, we lived in a rented house three blocks from the school where I would begin the third grade. My mother made friends with one of the neighbors, but one seemed enough for her. Within a year we would move again and, as she explained, there wasn't much point in getting too close to people we would have to say good-bye to. Our next house was less than a mile away, and the short journey would hardly merit tears or even good-byes, for that matter. It was more of a "see you later" situation, but still I adopted my mother's attitude, as it allowed me to pretend that not making friends was a conscious choice. I could if I wanted to. It just wasn't the right time.

Back in New York State, we had lived in the country, with no sidewalks or streetlights; you could leave the house and still be alone. But here, when you looked out the window, you saw other houses, and people inside those houses. I hoped that in walking around after dark I might witness a murder, but for the most part our neighbors just sat in their living rooms, watching TV. The only place that seemed truly different was owned by a man named Mr. Tomkey, who did not believe in television. This was told to us by our mother's friend, who dropped by one afternoon with a basketful of okra. The woman did not editorialize — rather, she just presented her information, leaving her listener to make of it what she might. Had my mother said, "That's the craziest thing I've ever heard in my life," I assume that the friend would have agreed, and had she said, "Three cheers for Mr. Tomkey," the friend likely would have agreed as well. It was a kind of test, as was the okra.

To say that you did not believe in television was different from saying that you did not care for it. Belief implied that television had a master plan and that you were against it. It also suggested that you thought too much. When my mother reported that Mr. Tomkey did not believe in television, my father said, "Well, good for him. I don't know that I believe in it, either."

"That's exactly how I feel," my mother said, and then my parents watched the news, and whatever came on after the news.

Word spread that Mr. Tomkey did not own a television, and you began hearing that while this was all very well and good, it was unfair of him to inflict his beliefs upon others, specifically his innocent wife and children. It was speculated that just as the blind man develops a keener sense of hearing, the family must somehow compensate for their loss. "Maybe they read," my mother's friend said. "Maybe they listen to the radio, but you can bet your boots they're doing *something*."

I wanted to know what this something was, and so I began peering through the Tomkeys' windows. During the day I'd stand across the street from their house, acting as though I were waiting for someone, and at night, when the view was better and I had less chance of being discovered, I would creep into their yard and hide in the bushes beside their fence.

Because they had no TV, the Tomkeys were forced to talk during dinner. They had no idea how puny their lives were, and so they were not ashamed that a camera would have found them uninteresting. They did not know what attractive was or what dinner was supposed to look like or even what time people were supposed to eat. Sometimes they wouldn't sit down until eight o'clock, long after everyone else had finished doing the dishes. During the meal, Mr. Tomkey would occasionally pound the table and point at his children with a fork, but the moment he finished, everyone would start laughing. I got the idea that he was imitating someone else, and wondered if he spied on us while we were eating.

When fall arrived and school began, I saw the Tomkey children marching up the hill with paper sacks in their hands. The son was one grade lower than me, and the daughter was one grade higher. We never spoke, but I'd pass them in the halls from time to time and attempt to view the world through their eyes. What must it be like to be so ignorant and alone? Could a normal person even imagine it? Staring at an Elmer Fudd lunch box, I tried to divorce myself from everything I already knew: Elmer's inability to pronounce the letter *r*, his constant pursuit of an intelligent and considerably more famous rabbit. I tried to think of him as just a drawing, but it was impossible to separate him from his celebrity.

One day in class a boy named William began to write the wrong answer on the blackboard, and our teacher flailed her arms, saying, "Warning, Will. Danger, danger." Her voice was synthetic and void of emotion, and we laughed, knowing that she was imitating the robot in a weekly show about a family who lived in outer space. The Tomkeys, though, would have thought she was having a heart attack. It occurred to me that they needed a guide, someone who could accompany them through the course of an average day and point out all the things they were unable to understand. I could have done it on weekends, but friendship would have taken away their mystery and interfered with the good feeling I got from pitying them. So I kept my distance.

In early October the Tomkeys bought a boat, and everyone seemed greatly relieved, especially my mother's friend, who noted that the motor was definitely secondhand. It was reported that Mr. Tomkey's father-in-law owned a house on the lake and had invited the family to use it whenever they liked. This explained why they were gone all weekend, but it did not make their absences any easier to bear. I felt as if my favorite show had been canceled.

Halloween fell on a Saturday that year, and by the time my mother took us to the store, all the good costumes were gone. My sisters dressed as witches and I went as a hobo. I'd looked forward to going in disguise to the Tomkeys' door, but they were off at the lake, and their house was dark. Before leaving, they had left a coffee can full of gumdrops on the front porch, alongside a sign reading DON'T BE GREEDY. In terms of Halloween candy, individual gumdrops were just about as low as you could get. This was evidenced by the large number of them floating in an adjacent dog bowl. It was disgusting to think that this was what a gumdrop might look like in your stomach, and it was insulting to be told not to take too much of something you didn't really want in the first place. "Who do these Tomkeys think they are?" my sister Lisa said.

The night after Halloween, we were sitting around watching TV when the doorbell rang. Visitors were infrequent at our house, so while my father stayed behind, my mother, sisters, and I ran downstairs in a group, opening the door to discover the entire Tomkey family on our front stoop. The parents looked as they always had, but the son and daughter were dressed in costumes — she as a ballerina and he as some kind of a rodent with terry-cloth ears and a tail made from what looked to be an extension cord. It seemed they had spent the previous evening isolated at the lake and had missed the opportunity to observe Halloween. "So, well, I guess we're trick-or-treating *now*, if that's okay," Mr. Tomkey said.

I attributed their behavior to the fact that they didn't have a TV, but television didn't teach you everything. Asking for candy on Halloween was called trick-or-treating, but asking for candy on November first was called begging, and it made people uncomfortable. This was one of the things you were supposed to learn simply by being alive, and it angered me that the Tomkeys did not understand it.

"Why of course it's not too late," my mother said. "Kids, why don't you . . . run and get . . . the candy."

"But the candy is gone," my sister Gretchen said. "You gave it away last night."

"Not *that* candy," my mother said. "The other candy. Why don't you run and go get it?"

"You mean *our* candy?" Lisa said. "The candy that we *earned?*"

This was exactly what our mother was talking about, but she didn't want to say this in front of the Tomkeys. In order to spare their feelings, she wanted them to believe that we always kept a bucket of candy lying around the house, just waiting for someone to knock on the door and ask for it. "Go on, now," she said. "Hurry up."

My room was situated right off the foyer, and if the Tomkeys had looked in that direction, they could have seen my bed and the

DAVID SEDARIS

brown paper bag marked MY CANDY. KEEP OUT. I didn't want them to know how much I had, and so I went into my room and shut the door behind me. Then I closed the curtains and emptied my bag onto the bed, searching for whatever was the crummiest. All my life chocolate has made me ill. I don't know if I'm allergic or what, but even the smallest amount leaves me with a blinding headache. Eventually, I learned to stay away from it, but as a child I refused to be left out. The brownies were eaten, and when the pounding began I would blame the grape juice or my mother's cigarette smoke or the tightness of my glasses — anything but the chocolate. My candy bars were poison but they were brand-name, and so I put them in pile no. 1, which definitely would not go to the Tomkeys.

Out in the hallway I could hear my mother straining for something to talk about. "A boat!" she said. "That sounds marvelous. Can you just drive it right into the water?"

"Actually, we have a trailer," Mr. Tomkey said. "So what we do is back it into the lake."

"Oh, a trailer. What kind is it?"

"Well, it's a *boat* trailer," Mr. Tomkey said.

"Right, but is it wooden or, you know . . . I guess what I'm asking is what *style* trailer do you have?"

Behind my mother's words were two messages. The first and most obvious was "Yes, I am talking about boat trailers, but also I am dying." The second, meant only for my sisters and me, was "If you do not immediately step forward with that candy, you will never again experience freedom, happiness, or the possibility of my warm embrace."

I knew that it was just a matter of time before she came into my room and started collecting the candy herself, grabbing indiscriminately, with no regard to my rating system. Had I been thinking straight, I would have hidden the most valuable items in my dresser drawer, but instead, panicked by the thought of her hand on my doorknob, I tore off the wrappers and began cramming the candy bars into my mouth, desperately, like someone in a contest. Most were miniature, which made them easier to accommodate, but still there was only so much room, and it was hard to chew and fit more in at the same time. The headache began immediately, and I chalked it up to tension.

My mother told the Tomkeys she needed to check on something, and then she opened the door and stuck her head inside my room. "What the *hell* are you doing?" she whispered, but my mouth was too full to answer. "I'll just be a moment," she called, and as she closed the door behind her and moved toward my bed, I began breaking the wax lips and candy necklaces pulled from pile no. 2. These were the second-best things I had received, and while it hurt to destroy them, it would have hurt even more to give them away. I had just started to mutilate a miniature box of Red Hots when my mother pried them from my hands, accidentally finishing the job for me. BB-size pellets clattered onto the floor, and as I followed them with my eyes, she snatched up a roll of Necco wafers.

"Not those," I pleaded, but rather than words, my mouth expelled chocolate, chewed chocolate, which fell onto the sleeve of her sweater. "Not those. Not those."

She shook her arm, and the mound of chocolate dropped like a horrible turd upon my bedspread. "You should look at yourself," she said. "I mean, *really* look at yourself."

Along with the Necco wafers she took several Tootsie Pops and half a dozen caramels wrapped in cellophane. I heard her apologize to the Tomkeys for her absence, and then I heard my candy hitting the bottom of their bags.

"What do you say?" Mrs. Tomkey asked.

And the children answered, "Thank you."

While I was in trouble for not bringing my candy sooner, my sisters were in more trouble for not bringing theirs at all. We spent the early part of the evening in our rooms, then one by one we eased our way back upstairs, and joined our parents in front of the TV. I was the last to arrive, and took a seat on the floor beside the sofa. The show was a Western, and even if my head had not been throbbing, I doubt I would have had the wherewithal to follow it. A posse of outlaws crested a rocky hilltop, squinting at a flurry of dust advancing from the horizon, and I thought again of the Tomkeys and of how alone and out of place they had looked in their dopey costumes. "What was up with that kid's tail?" I asked.

"Shhhh," my family said.

For months I had protected and watched over these people, but now, with one stupid act, they had turned my pity into something hard and ugly. The shift wasn't gradual, but immediate, and it provoked an uncomfortable feeling of loss. We hadn't been friends, the Tomkeys and I, but still I had given them the gift of my curiosity. Wondering about the Tomkey family had made me feel generous, but now I would have to shift gears and find pleasure in hating them. The only alternative was to do as my mother had instructed and take a good look at myself. This was an old trick, designed to turn one's hatred inward, and while I was determined not to fall for it, it was hard to shake the mental picture snapped by her suggestion: here is a boy sitting on a bed, his mouth smeared with chocolate. He's a human being, but also he's a pig, surrounded by trash and gorging himself so that others may be denied. Were this the only image in the world, you'd be forced to give it your full attention, but fortunately there were others. This stagecoach, for instance, coming round the bend with a cargo of gold. This shiny new Mustang convertible. This teenage girl, her hair a beautiful mane, sipping Pepsi through a straw, one picture after another, on and on until the news, and whatever came on after the news.

Let It Snow

In Binghamton, New York, winter meant snow, and though I was young when we left, I was able to recall great heaps of it, and use that memory as evidence that North Carolina was, at best, a third-rate institution. What little snow there was would usually melt an hour or two after hitting the ground, and there you'd be in your windbreaker and unconvincing mittens, forming a lumpy figure made mostly of mud. Snow Negroes, we called them.

The winter I was in the fifth grade we got lucky. Snow fell, and for the first time in years, it accumulated. School was canceled and two days later we got lucky again. There were eight inches on the ground, and rather than melting, it froze. On the fifth day of our vacation my mother had a little breakdown. Our presence had disrupted the secret life she led while we were at school, and when she could no longer take it she threw us out. It wasn't a gentle request, but something closer to an eviction. "Get the hell out of my house," she said.

We reminded her that it was our house, too, and she opened the front door and shoved us into the carport. "And stay out!" she shouted.

My sisters and I went down the hill and sledded with other children from the neighborhood. A few hours later we returned home, surprised to find that the door was still locked. "Oh, come on," we said. I rang the bell and when no one answered we went to the window and saw our mother in the kitchen, watching television. Normally she waited until five o'clock to have a drink, but for the past few days she'd been making an exception. Drinking didn't count if you followed a glass of wine with a cup of coffee, and so she had both a goblet and a mug positioned before her on the countertop.

"Hey!" we yelled. "Open the door. It's us." We knocked on the pane, and without looking in our direction, she refilled her goblet and left the room.

"That bitch," my sister Lisa said. We pounded again and again, and when our mother failed to answer we went around back and threw snowballs at her bedroom window. "You are going to be in so much trouble when Dad gets home!" we shouted, and in response my mother pulled the drapes. Dusk approached, and as it grew colder it occurred to us that we could possibly die. It happened, surely. Selfish mothers wanted the house to themselves, and their children were discovered years later, frozen like mastodons in blocks of ice.

My sister Gretchen suggested that we call our father, but none of us knew his number, and he probably wouldn't have done anything anyway. He'd gone to work specifically to escape our mother, and between the weather and her mood, it could be hours or even days before he returned home.

"One of us should get hit by a car," I said. "That would teach the both of them." I pictured Gretchen, her life hanging by a thread as my parents paced the halls of Rex Hospital, wishing they had been more attentive. It was really the perfect solution. With her out of the way, the rest of us would be more valuable and have a bit more room to spread out. "Gretchen, go lie in the street."

"Make Amy do it," she said.

Amy, in turn, pushed it off onto Tiffany, who was the youngest and had no concept of death. "It's like sleeping," we told her. "Only you get a canopy bed."

Poor Tiffany. She'd do just about anything in return for a little affection. All you had to do was call her Tiff and whatever you wanted was yours: her allowance money, her dinner, the contents of her Easter basket. Her eagerness to please was absolute and naked. When we asked her to lie in the middle of the street, her only question was "Where?"

We chose a quiet dip between two hills, a spot where drivers were almost required to skid out of control. She took her place, this six-year-old in a butter-colored coat, and we gathered on the curb to watch. The first car to happen by belonged to a neighbor, a fellow Yankee who had outfitted his tires with chains and stopped a few feet from our sister's body. "Is that a person?" he asked.

"Well, sort of," Lisa said. She explained that we'd been locked out of our house and though the man appeared to accept it as a reasonable explanation, I'm pretty sure it was him who told on us. Another car passed and then we saw our mother, this puffy figure awkwardly negotiating the crest of the hill. She did not own a pair of pants, and her legs were buried to the calves in snow. We wanted to send her home, to kick her out of nature just as she had kicked us out of the house, but it was hard to stay angry at someone that pitiful-looking.

"Are you wearing your *loafers*?" Lisa asked, and in response our mother raised her bare foot. "I *was* wearing loafers," she said. "I mean, really, it was there a second ago."

This was how things went. One moment she was locking us out of our own house and the next we were rooting around in the snow, looking for her left shoe. "Oh, forget about it," she said. "It'll turn up in a few days." Gretchen fitted her cap over my mother's foot. Lisa secured it with her scarf, and surrounding her tightly on all sides, we made our way back home.

DAVID SEDARIS

Six to Eight Black Men

I've never been much for guidebooks, so when trying to get my bearings in some strange American city, I normally start by asking the cabdriver or hotel clerk some silly question regarding the latest census figures. I say "silly" because I don't really *care* how many people live in Olympia, Washington, or Columbus, Ohio. They're nice-enough places, but the numbers mean nothing to me. My second question might have to do with the average annual rainfall, which, again, doesn't tell me anything about the people who have chosen to call this place home.

What really interests me are the local gun laws. Can I carry a concealed weapon and, if so, under what circumstances? What's the waiting period for a tommy gun? Could I buy a Glock 17 if I were recently divorced or fired from my job? I've learned from experience that it's best to lead into this subject as delicately as possible, especially if you and the local citizen are alone and enclosed in a relatively small area. Bide your time, though, and you can walk away with some excellent stories. I've learned, for example, that the blind can legally hunt in both Texas and Michigan. In Texas they must be accompanied by a sighted companion, but I heard that in Michigan they're allowed to go it alone, which raises the question: How do they find whatever it is they just shot? In addition to that, how do they get it home? Are the Michigan blind allowed to drive as well? I ask about guns not because I want one of my own but because the answers vary so widely from state to state. In a country that's become increasingly homogeneous, I'm reassured by these last charming touches of regionalism.

Firearms aren't really an issue in Europe, so when traveling abroad, my first question usually relates to barnyard animals. "What do your roosters say?" is a good icebreaker, as every country has its own unique interpretation. In Germany, where dogs bark "vow vow" and both the frog and the duck say "quack," the rooster greets the dawn with a hearty "kik-a-riki." Greek roosters crow "kiri-a-kee," and in France they scream "coco-rico," which sounds like one of those horrible premixed cocktails with a pirate on the label. When told that an American rooster says "cock-a-doodle-doo," my hosts look at me with disbelief and pity.

"When do you open your Christmas presents?" is another good conversation starter, as I think it explains a lot about national character. People who traditionally open gifts on Christmas Eve seem a bit more pious and family-oriented than those who wait until Christmas morning. They go to Mass, open presents, eat a late meal, return to church the following morning, and devote the rest of the day to eating another big meal. Gifts are generally reserved for children, and the parents tend not to go overboard. It's nothing I'd want for myself, but I suppose it's fine for those who prefer food and family to things of real value.

In France and Germany gifts are exchanged on Christmas Eve, while in the Netherlands the children open their presents on December 5, in celebration of St. Nicholas Day. It sounded sort of quaint until I spoke to a man named Oscar, who filled me in on a few of the details as we walked from my hotel to the Amsterdam train station.

Unlike the jolly, obese American Santa, Saint Nicholas is painfully thin and dresses not unlike the pope, topping his robes with a tall hat resembling an embroidered tea cozy. The outfit, I was told, is a carryover from his former career, when he served as the bishop of Turkey.

"I'm sorry," I said, "but could you repeat that?"

One doesn't want to be too much of a cultural chauvinist, but this seemed completely wrong to me. For starters, Santa didn't *used to do* anything. He's not retired and, more important, he has nothing to do with Turkey. It's too dangerous there, and the people wouldn't appreciate him. When asked how he got from Turkey to the North Pole, Oscar told me with complete conviction that Saint Nicholas currently resides in Spain, which again is simply not true. Though he could probably live wherever he wanted, Santa chose the North Pole specifically because it is harsh and isolated. No one can spy on him, and he doesn't have to worry about people coming to the door. Anyone can come to the door in Spain, and in that outfit he'd most certainly be recognized. On top of that, aside from a few pleasantries, Santa doesn't speak Spanish. "Hello. How are you? Can I get you some candy?" Fine. He knows enough to get by, but he's not fluent and he certainly doesn't eat tapas.

While our Santa flies in on a sled, the Dutch version arrives by boat and then transfers to a white horse. The event is televised, and great crowds gather at the waterfront to greet him. I'm not sure if there's a set date, but he generally docks in late November and spends a few weeks hanging out and asking people what they want.

"Is it just him alone?" I asked. "Or does he come with some backup?"

Oscar's English was close to perfect, but he seemed thrown by a term normally reserved for police reinforcement.

"Helpers," I said. "Does he have any elves?"

Maybe I'm overly sensitive, but I couldn't help but feel personally insulted when Oscar denounced the very idea as grotesque and unrealistic. "Elves," he said. "They are just so silly."

The words *silly* and *unrealistic* were redefined when I learned that Saint Nicholas travels with what was consistently described as "six to eight black men." I asked several Dutch people to narrow it down, but none of them could give me an exact number. It was always "six to eight," which seems strange, seeing as they've had hundreds of years to get an accurate head count.

The six to eight black men were characterized as personal slaves until the mid-1950s, when the political climate changed and it was decided that instead of being slaves they were just good friends. I think history has proved that something usually comes *between* slavery and friendship, a period of time marked not by cookies and quiet hours beside the fire but by bloodshed and mutual hostility. They have such violence in the Netherlands, but rather than duking it out amongst themselves, Santa and his former slaves decided to take it out on the public. In the early years if a child was naughty, Saint Nicholas and the six to eight black men would beat him with what Oscar described as "the small branch of a tree."

"A switch?"

"Yes," he said. "That's it. They'd kick him and beat him with a switch. Then if the youngster was really bad, they'd put him in a sack and take him back to Spain."

"Saint Nicholas would *kick* you?"

"Well, not anymore," Oscar said. "Now he just *pretends* to kick you."

He considered this to be progressive, but in a way I think it's almost more perverse than the original punishment. "I'm going to hurt you but not really." How many times have we fallen for that line? The fake slap invariably makes contact, adding the elements of shock and betrayal to what had previously been plain old-fashioned fear. What kind of a Santa spends his time pretending to kick people before stuffing them into a canvas sack? Then, of course, you've got the six to eight former slaves who could potentially go off at any moment. This, I think, is the greatest difference between us and the Dutch. While a certain segment of our population might be perfectly happy with the arrangement, if you told the average white American that six to eight nameless black men would be sneaking into his house in the middle of the night, he would barricade the doors and arm himself with whatever he could get his hands on.

"*Six to eight*, did you say?"

In the years before central heating, Dutch children would leave their shoes by the fireplace, the promise being that unless they planned to beat you, kick you, or stuff you into a sack, Saint Nicholas and the six to eight black men would fill your clogs with presents. Aside from the threats of violence and kidnapping, it's not much different than hanging your stockings from the mantel. Now that so few people actually have a working fireplace, Dutch children are instructed to leave their shoes beside the radiator, furnace, or space heater. Saint Nicholas and the six to eight black men arrive on horses, which jump from the yard onto the roof. At this point I guess they either jump back down and use the door or stay put and vaporize through the pipes and electrical cords. Oscar wasn't too clear about the particulars, but really, who can blame him? We have the same problem with our Santa. He's supposed to use the chimney, but if you don't have one, he still manages to get in. It's best not to think about it too hard.

While eight flying reindeer are a hard pill to swallow, our Christmas story remains relatively dull. Santa lives with his wife in a remote polar village and spends one night a year traveling around the world. If you're bad, he leaves you coal. If you're good and live in America, he'll give you just about anything you want. We tell our children to be good and send them off to bed, where they lie awake, anticipating their great bounty. A Dutch parent has a decidedly hairier story to relate, telling his children, "Listen, you might want to pack a few of your things together before going to bed. The former bishop of Turkey will be coming tonight along with six to eight black men. They might put some candy in your shoes, they might stuff you into a sack and take you to Spain, or they might just pretend to kick you. We don't know for sure, but we want you to be prepared."

This is the reward for living in the Netherlands. As a child you get to hear this story, and as an adult you get to turn around and repeat it. As an added bonus, the government has thrown in legalized drugs and prostitution — so what's *not* to love about being Dutch?

Oscar finished his story just as we arrived at the station. He was an amiable guy — very good company — but when he offered to wait until my train arrived I begged off, claiming I had some calls to make. Sitting alone in the vast, vibrant terminal, surrounded by thousands of polite, seemingly interesting Dutch people, I couldn't help but feel second-rate. Yes, the Netherlands was a small country, but it had six to eight black men and a really good bedtime story. Being a fairly competitive person, I felt jealous, then bitter. I was edging toward hostile when I remembered the blind hunter tramping off alone into the Michigan forest. He may bag a deer, or he may happily shoot a camper in the stomach. He may find his way back to the car, or he may wander around for a week or two before stumbling through your back door. We don't know for sure, but in pinning that license to his chest, he inspires the sort of narrative that ultimately makes me proud to be an American.

The Monster Mash

The thing about dead people is that they look really dead, fake almost, like models made of wax. This I learned at the medical examiner's office I visited in the fall of 1997. While the bodies seemed unreal, the tools used to pick them apart were disturbingly familiar. It might be different in places with better funding, but here the pathologists used hedge clippers to snip through rib cages. Chest cavities were emptied of blood with cheap metal soup ladles, the kind you'd see in cafeterias, and the autopsy tables were lubricated with whatever dish detergent happened to be on sale. Also familiar were the songs, oldies mainly, that issued from the blood-spattered radio and formed a kind of sound track. When I was young, I associated Three Dog Night with my seventh-grade shop teacher, who proudly identified himself as the group's biggest fan. Now, though, whenever I hear "Joy to the World," I think of a fibroid tumor positioned upon a Styrofoam plate. Funny how that happens.

While at the medical examiner's office, I dressed in a protective suit, complete with a bonnet and a pair of Tyvek booties. Citizens were disemboweled, one right after another, and on the surface I'm sure I seemed fine with it. Then at night I'd return to my hotel, double-lock the door, and stand under the shower until all the soap and shampoo were used up. The people in the next room must have wondered what was going on. An hour of running water, and then this blubbery voice: "I do believe in spooks, I do believe in spooks, I do, I do, I do, I do, I do."

It's not as if I'd walked into this completely unprepared. Even as a child I was fascinated by death, not in a spiritual sense, but in an aesthetic one. A hamster or guinea pig would pass away, and, after burying the body, I'd dig it back up: over and over, until all that remained was a shoddy pelt. It earned me a certain reputation, especially when I moved on to other people's pets. "Igor," they called me. "Wicked, spooky." But I think my interest was actually fairly common, at least among adolescent boys. At that age, death is something that happens only to animals and grandparents, and studying it is like a science project, the good kind that doesn't involve homework. Most kids grow out of it, but the passing of time only heightened my curiosity.

As a young man, I saved up my dishwashing money and bought a seventy-five-dollar copy of *Medicolegal Investigations of*

Death, a sort of bible for forensic pathologists. It shows what you might look like if you bit an extension cord while standing in a shallow pool of water, if you were crushed by a tractor, struck by lightning, strangled with a spiral or nonspiral telephone cord, hit with a claw hammer, burned, shot, drowned, stabbed, or feasted upon by wild or domestic animals. The captions read like really great poem titles, my favorite being "Extensive Mildew on the Face of a Recluse." I stared at that picture for hours on end, hoping it might inspire me, but I know nothing about poetry, and the best I came up with was pretty lame:

> *Behold the recluse looking pensive!*
> *Mildew, though, is quite extensive*
> *On his head, both aft and fore.*
> *He maybe shoulda got out more.*

I know nothing about biology either. The pathologists tried to educate me, but I was too distracted by the grotesque: my discovery, for instance, that if you jump from a tall building and land on your back, your eyes will pop out of your head and hang by bloody cables. "Like those joke glasses!" I said to the chief medical examiner. The man was nothing if not professional, and his response to my observations was always the same: "Well." He'd sigh. "Not really."

After a week in the autopsy suite, I still couldn't open a Denny's menu without wanting to throw up. At night I'd close my eyes and see the buckets of withered hands stored in the office's secondary cooler. The cooler contained brains too, a whole wall of them shelved like preserves in a general store. Then there were the bits and pieces: a forsaken torso, a pretty blond scalp, a pair of eyes floating in a baby food jar. Put them all together, and you had an incredibly bright secretary who could type like the wind but never answer the telephone. I'd lie awake thinking of things like this, but then my mind would return to the freshly dead, who were most often whole, or at least whole-*ish*.

Most of the them were delivered naked, zipped up in identical body bags. Family members were not allowed inside the building, and so the corpses had no context. Unconnected to the living, they were like these strange creatures, related only to one another. A police report would explain that Mrs. Daniels had been killed when a truck lost control and drove through the front window of a hamburger stand, where she had been waiting in line for her order. But that was it in terms of a narrative. Did the victim have children? Was there a Mr. Daniels? How was it that she found herself at this particular hamburger stand on this particular afternoon? In cases like hers, I needed more than a standard report. There had to be a reason this woman was run down, as, without one, the same thing might happen to me. Three men are shot to death while attending a child's christening, and you tell yourself, *Sure. They were hanging out with the wrong crowd.* But buying a hamburger? *I* buy hamburgers. Or I used to, anyway.

This medical examiner's office was in the western United States, in a city where guns are readily available and drivers are known to shoot each other over parking spaces. The building was low-slung and mean-looking, set on the far edge of the downtown area, between the railroad tracks and a rubber stamp manufacturer. In the lobby was a potted plant and a receptionist who kept a can of Mountain Glen air freshener in her desk drawer. "For decomps," she explained, meaning those who had died alone and rotted awhile before being found. We had such a case on Halloween, an eighty-year-old man who had tumbled from a ladder while replacing a lightbulb. Four and a half days on the floor of his un-air-conditioned home, and as the bag was unzipped the room filled with what the attending pathologist termed "the smell of job security." The autopsy took place in the morning and was the best argument for the buddy system I had ever seen. *Never live alone*, I told myself. *Before you change a lightbulb, call someone from the other room and have him watch until you are finished.*

By this point in my stay, my list of don'ts covered three pages and included such reminders as: never fall asleep in a Dumpster, never underestimate a bee, never drive a convertible behind a flatbed truck, never get old, never get drunk near a train, and never, under any circumstances, cut off your air supply while masturbating. This last one is a nationwide epidemic, and it's surprising the number of men who do it while dressed in their wife's clothing, most often while she is out of town. To anyone with similar inclinations, a word of warning: after you're discovered, the police will take snapshots of your dead, costumed body, which will then be slid into photo albums and pored over by people like me, who can't take the stench of an incoming decomp, so hole themselves up in the records room, moaning, "Oh, my God. Oh, my God. Oh, my God," not sure if they're referring to your plum-colored face or to the squash blossom necklace you've chosen to go with that blouse.

I hadn't timed my visit to coincide with Halloween, but that's the way it worked out. You'd think that most of the casualties would involve children, trick-or-treaters hit by cars or done in by tainted candy, but actually the day was just like any other. In the morning we had our decomposed senior, and after lunch I accompanied a female pathologist to a murder trial. She had performed the victim's autopsy and was testifying on behalf of the prosecution. There were plenty of things that should have concerned me—the blood-spatter evidence, the trajectory of the bullets—but all I could concentrate on was the defendant's mother, who'd come to court wearing cutoff jeans and a *Ghostbusters* T-shirt. It couldn't have been easy for her, but still you had to wonder: what *would* she consider a dress-up occasion?

After the trial, I watched as another female pathologist collected maggots from a spinal column found in the desert. There was a decomposed head, too, and before leaving work she planned to simmer it and study the exposed cranium for contusions. I was asked to pass this information along to the chief medical examiner, and, looking back, I perhaps should have chosen my words more carefully. "Fire up the kettle," I told him. "Ol'-fashioned skull boil at five P.M."

It was, of course, the fear talking, that and a pathetic desire to appear casual, one of the gang. That evening, instead of returning to my hotel, I sat around with the transporters, one of whom had recently been ticketed for using the car pool lane and had argued, unsuccessfully, that the dead body he was carrying in the back constituted a second passenger. I'd thought these guys would be morose and scary-looking, the type who live in basements and have no social skills, but they were actually just the opposite. Several of them had worked for undertakers, and told me that gypsy funerals were the worst. "They set up in the parking lot, tap into the electricity, and grill chicken until, like, forever." They recalled finding the eye of a suicide victim stuck to the bottom of a bedroom door, and then they turned on the TV and started watching a horror movie, which I can't believe had any real effect on them.

It was just the four of us until around midnight, when a tipsy man in a Daytona Beach sweatshirt came to the front gate and asked for a tour. When the transporters refused him, he gestured toward an idling car and got his girlfriend to ask. The young woman was lovely and flirtatious, and as she pressed herself against the gate I imagined her lying upon an autopsy table, her organs piled in a glistening heap beside her. I now looked at everyone this way, and it worried me that I'd never be able to stop. This was the consequence of seeing too much and understanding the horrible truth: No one is safe. The world is not manageable. The trick-or-treater may not be struck down on Halloween, but sooner or later he is going to get it, as am I, and everyone I have ever cared about.

It goes without saying that for the next few weeks I was not much fun to live with. In early November, I returned home and re-pelled every single person I came into contact with. Gradually, though, my gloominess wore off. By Thanksgiving I was imagining people naked rather than dead and naked, which was an improve-ment. A week later, I was back to smoking in bed, and, just as I thought that I'd put it all behind me, I went to my neighborhood grocery store and saw an elderly woman slip on a grape. She fell hard, and after running to her side I took her by the arm. "You really have to watch yourself in this produce aisle."

"I know it," she said. "I could have broken my leg."

"Actually," I told her, "you could have been killed."

The woman attempted to stand, but I wouldn't let her. "I'm se-rious. People die this way. I've seen it."

Her expression changed then, becoming fearful rather than merely pained. It was the look you get when facing a sudden and insurmountable danger: the errant truck, the shaky ladder, the crazy person who pins you to the linoleum and insists, with in-creasing urgency, that everything you know and love can be un-done by a grape.

The Cow and the Turkey

T he cow was notoriously cheap, so it surprised everyone when she voted yes for the secret Santa scheme. It was the horse's suggestion and she backed it immediately, saying, "I choose the turkey."

The pig, who considered himself an authority on all things gifty, cleared his throat. "That's not actually the way it works," he said. "It's secret, see, so we each draw a name and keep it to ourselves until Christmas morning."

"Why do you always have to be like that?" the cow asked, and the duck sighed, "Here we go."

"First you ask me to give someone a Christmas present," the cow continued, "and then you tell me it has to be done *your* way. Like, 'Oh, I have four legs so I'm better than everyone else.'"

"Don't *you* have four legs?" the pig asked.

The cow loosed something between a moan and a sigh. "All right, just because you have a curly tail," she said.

The pig tried looking behind him, but all he could see were his sides. "Is it curly *curly*?" he asked the rooster. "Or curly *kinky*?"

"The point is that I'm tired of being pushed around," the cow said. "I think a lot of us are."

This was her all over, so rather than spending the next week listening to her complain, it was decided that the cow would give to the turkey, and that everyone else would keep their names a secret.

There were, of course, no shops in the barnyard, which was a shame, as all of the animals had money, coins mainly, dropped by the farmer and his plump, moody children as they went about their chores. The cow once had close to three dollars, and gave it to a calf the family was taking into town. "I want you to buy me a knapsack," she'd told him. "Just like the one the farmer's daughter has, only bigger and blue instead of green. Can you remember that?"

The calf had tucked the money into his cheek before being led out of the barn. "And wouldn't you know it," the cow later complained, "isn't it just my luck that he never came back?"

She'd spent the first few days of his absence in a constant, almost giddy state of anticipation. Watching the barn door, listening for the sound of the truck, waiting for that knapsack, something that would belong only to her.

When it no longer made sense to hope, she turned to self-pity, then rage. The calf had taken advantage of her, had spent her precious money on a bus ticket and boarded thinking, *So long, sucker.*

It was a consolation, then, to overhear the farmer talking to his wife and learn that "taking an animal into town" was a euphemism for hitting him in the head with an electric hammer. *So long, sucker.*

Milking put the cow in close proximity to humans, much closer than any of the other animals, and she learned a lot by keeping her ears open: who was dating whom, how much it cost to fill a gas tank, any number of useful little tidbits — menu for Christmas dinner, for instance. The family had spent Thanksgiving visiting the farmer's mother in her retirement home and had eaten what tasted like potato chips soaked in chicken fat. Now they were going to make up for it, "big time," the farmer's wife said, "and with all the trimmings."

The turkey didn't know that he would be killed on Christmas Eve; no one knew except the cow. That's why she'd specifically chosen his name for the secret Santa program — it got her off the hook and made tolerable his constant, fidgety enthusiasm.

"You'll never in a million years guess what I got you," she said to him a day after the names were drawn.

"Is it a bath mat?" the turkey asked. He'd seen one hanging on the farmer's clothesline and was promptly, senselessly, taken by it. "It's a towel for the floor!" he kept telling everyone. "I mean, really, isn't that just the greatest idea you've ever heard in your life?"

"Oh, this is a lot better than a bath mat," the cow said, chuckling as the turkey sputtered, "No way!" and "What could possibly be better than a bath mat?"

"You'll see come Christmas morning," she told him.

Most of the animals were giving food as their secret Santa gift. No one came out and actually said it, but the cow had noticed them setting a little aside, not just scraps, but the best parts — the horse her oats, the pig his thick crusts of bread. Even the rooster, who was the biggest glutton of all, had managed to sacrifice and had stockpiled a fistful of grain behind an empty gas can in the far corner of the barn. He and the others were surely hungry, yet none of them complained about it. And this bothered the cow more than anything. *Which of you is sacrificing for me?* she wondered, her mouth watering at the thought of a treat. She looked at the pig, who sat smiling in his pen, and then at the turkey, who'd hung a sprig of mistletoe from the end of his wattle and was waltzing from one animal to the next, saying, "Any takers?" Even to other guys.

Oh, how his cheerfulness grated on her. Waiting for Christmas Eve was murder, but wait the cow did, and when the time was right — just shortly after breakfast — she sidled up beside him.

"You do know they'll be cutting your head off, don't you?" she whispered.

The turkey offered his strange half-smile, the one that said both "You're kidding" and "Please tell me you're kidding."

"If it's not the farmer it'll be one of his children," the cow explained. "The middle one, probably, the boy with the earring. There were some jokes about doing it with a chain saw, but if I know them they'll stick to the ax. It's more traditional."

The turkey laughed, deciding it was a joke, but then he saw the pleasure in the cow's face and knew that she was telling the truth.

"How long have you known?" he asked.

"A few weeks," the cow told him. "I meant to tell you earlier, but with all the excitement, I guess I forgot."

"Kill me *and* eat me?"

The cow nodded.

The turkey pulled the mistletoe from the end of his wattle. "Well, golly," he said. "Don't I feel stupid."

Not wanting to spoil anyone's Christmas, the turkey announced that he would be spending the holiday with relatives. "The wild side of the family," he said. "Just flew in last night from Kentucky." Noon arrived, and when the farmer and his middle son appeared in the barnyard, the turkey went to them without a fuss, saying, "So long everyone" and "See you in a few days."

They all waved good-bye except for the cow, who lowered her head toward her empty trough. She was just thinking that a little extra food might be nice, when something horrible occurred to her. The rooster was standing in the doorway, and she almost trampled him on her way outside shouting, "Wait! Come back. Whose name did you draw?"

"Say what?" the turkey said.

"I said, whose name did you get? Who's supposed to receive your secret Santa present?"

The turkey answered a thin, "You'll see," his voice a little song that hung in the air long after he'd disappeared.

David Sedaris's half-dozen books have been translated into twenty-five languages, including Estonian, Greek, and Bahasa. His essays appear frequently in *The New Yorker* and are heard on Public Radio International's *This American Life*.